Janet Frame

was born in Dunedin, New Zealand, in 1924. She has written more than ten novels, five collections of short stories, a volume of poetry and a children's book. Her novel, *The Carpathians*, won the Commonwealth Prize for literature in 1989, and her three-volume autobiography was made into a much-acclaimed film, *An Angel at My Table*, by fellow New Zealander, Jane Campion, in 1991. Janet Frame has won a number of distinctions in her native country and was awarded a CBE in 1983.

By the same author

Novels

OWLS DO CRY
FACES IN THE WATER
THE EDGE OF THE ALPHABET
SCENTED GARDENS FOR THE BLIND
THE ADAPTABLE MAN
A STATE OF SIEGE
THE RAINBIRDS
INTENSIVE CARE
DAUGHTER BUFFALO
LIVING IN MANIOTOTO
THE CARPATHIANS
YELLOW FLOWERS IN THE ANTIPODEAN ROOM

Stories and Sketches

THE LAGOON
THE RESERVOIR
SNOWMAN SNOWMAN
YOU ARE NOW ENTERING THE HUMAN HEART

For Children

MONO MINIM AND THE SMELL OF THE SUN

Poetry

THE POCKET MIRROR

Autobiography

TO THE IS-LAND
AN ANGEL AT MY TABLE
THE ENVOY FROM MIRROR CITY

JANET FRAME

Daughter Buffalo

Flamingo
An Imprint of HarperCollinsPublishers

Flamingo
An Imprint of HarperCollins*Publishers*
77–85 Fulham Palace Road,
Hammersmith, London W6 8JB

Published by Flamingo 1993
9 8 7 6 5 4 3 2 1

First published in Great Britain by
Pandora Press 1990

ISBN 0 00 654614 5

Set in Goudy

Printed in Great Britain by
The Guernsey Press Co. Ltd, Guernsey, Channel Islands

Grateful acknowledgement to
Sue and John Marquand,
John Money,
and the Yaddo Corporation,
for their hospitality

Mice are not men, everyone is happily saying.
Then why are the mice praying?

Men are not Gods, everyone was saying
when the mice began praying to the men.

Out of this mixture, why say No No
to my daughter, the bewildered buffalo?

—Turnlung

CONTENTS

Prologue   xi

PART ONE   D.   3

PART TWO   The Bees in the Flowering Currant   25

PART THREE   Down Instant Street, Jewels, and The Finishing Touch   77

PART FOUR   Man, Dog, Buffalo, Do You Know Your Name?   165

Epilogue   209

PROLOGUE

I am Turnlung.
Soon I shall give up the first and secondhand furniture of
    memory.
I shall live in a hollow house
listening to the glint of the sun.

The surfaces of life still adhere to me.
I am contained in the orange and lemon trees in my garden,
the brown rush matting on the floor of my living room.
Rain stops on my face. Bees, passing, pick up salt and honey
    from my skin.
I have a constant coming and going of breath.

Soon my life will run out like the fluids of my body.
I shall be among the dead great and small,
a composite heart of man woman and beast,
free of the stone-dust and the honey.

The beach is near. The days are distant traffic.
I'm stopped. I'm going nowhere.
Death will make corrupting changes, will tamper;
we shall be lovers lying tuned at last,
blended in due proportion,
squamata, sauria, serpentes.
Dog-heart, buffalo progeny,
the bestial sun spoiling in secret,
the pink-skinned white mice put genetically in tune.

I'm old; I may be slightly mad.
My weather is mostly moderate.
I can still walk and think and write.
I fear and love. I look out
at the noon tides of water and grass,
at the people, the animals burying their faces in a blossom
of
   ocean and earth,
in the heliocentric place of stone light.

DAUGHTER
BUFFALO

PART ONE

D.

1

I am Talbot Edelman, medical graduate, a student of death, writing of a time now or long past which appears as a dream though I am not a dreaming kind of man. Let me tell you about myself and my experiences of three weeks of one summer.

I was brought up on Long Island in a comparatively new house with plenty of space and clear air and with neighbours viewed with tolerance through trees, the noble allies of tolerance. We were a smooth rich family: smooth, rich and clean. My father owned a profitable business, manufacturing small articles—hairclips, paperclips, pens, coat hangers, and other 'notions'— but as few references to his business were made in our home and as it was his custom each weekend to bring home a painting he had bought, I used to think of him as a picture dealer rather than as a businessman. He would hang the paintings at home or offer them on loan to a museum. They were 'safe' paintings, never fashionable, always pleasant, usually full of curves, smiles and summer colours, and my father loved each new one more than the last, for each, to him was like an instalment of hope.

'I think it's fine,' he would say. 'Look at the colour. It could be a Cézanne.'

He bought paintings that could be but never were, and in this they were company for him. When I learned to see him through adult eyes I knew that he was a man who could have been but never was what his dreams had planned for him, and I was grateful that he never used me, his elder son, nor my young brother Benjamin, at business college, as instruments to give birth to the reality of his dreams.

The remaining member of our family was Mother, an intelligent pretty woman who kept a kitchen like a jet control room full of throbbing whirring grinding machines flashing with time-lights and heat-lights. I was very fond of my mother.

At home, between semesters, my brother and I would talk confidently and comfortably of how we planned to spend our generous allowance, of the next car we hoped to buy, of the countries we would visit during our next vacation. Our voices as we talked were rich with certainty. If appearances mattered most—being beautiful and handsome, walking gracefully from room to room, furnishing a pleasant house in a pleasant manner, smiling at one another through breakfast, lunch, dinner, sharing music, books, paintings, being ambitious and talking freely of our ambitions—then we should have been on display as an ideal family. Guests who came to stay for the weekend would leave almost with tears in their eyes as they said, 'We've never been in a house so full of peace and love.'

I felt this to be true. In our home everyone was loved, everything was loved—the family, the furniture, the rugs on the floors, the books, the paintings, even the bathroom fittings. We delighted in the benefits of education and moderate wealth. We were good citizens of our country and of the world. We contributed to charity, my father willingly took his place when called for jury duty, and I'm sure he brought wisdom and consideration to the settlement of disputes.

You may wonder why, in the midst of this apparent perfection, I chose to specialise in the study of death.

For years without success I searched for Death in my own home. I gradually learned that just as people refuse to accept the knowledge of the anatomy of their own bodies (ask any anatomy professor about the resistance shown by students toward learning to name the parts of their body), so they are reluctant to include the experience of death in their lives, regarding it until the end as their last guaranteed immunity. They start early. With each death among their friends and family they do not more readily accept the idea of their own death; they merely dose themselves with a vaccine obtained from each death, renewing their own immunity year after year with the help of the dead until, although they may have reached an age when few of their own generation have survived, they still assure themselves of their own invulnerability. Finally, over-immunised, they catch the infection and give up the ghost, and their death is harder for them if they have been taught to fight every natural process as they fought, at first, against breathing. They must learn to work toward a constant treason of their will.

I learned little of this from my own home. Our garbage was removed by an automatic disposal unit. Everyone took many baths, drying with thirsty towels which in their turn played the family game by seeming to render invisible all traces of hair, stains of living, dust, sweat. All our happy conversations, our plans lovingly composed together, had no mention of death. In winter when the snow was deep and the year's leaves had died and were buried, when only a few creatures—squirrels, cardinals, crows— could be seen, you might have imagined that even we would be tempted or persuaded to surrender ourselves or part of ourselves to the surrounding death-light, to perceive its shadow in our faces, to take time to consider the silence and the peace, for we were a thoughtful family, and we knew about darkness, and surely our parents met it in their loving as we met it in our childhood tears and happinesses. Yet each winter we let pass the opportunity to invite death as a rightful guest, without fuss, into our home, and before we knew it the trees had new leaves, the sun melted the iron bars of the winter prison, and death unfrozen flew away as a scarlet bird, a golden bee or fly, as if it had never been; and for us, it had not; for us, the sun was like money, always with us and in use. Should death wish to be near us our unspoken mutual agreement kept it at a safe distance—within the paintings and books and music from which it was forbidden to burst.

What control we had over our world!

I remember my shock when I learned that my father had been brought up in a Jewish ghetto in Brooklyn. He had become so separated from his early life that there was little trace of it; he had used the clean garbage disposal unit on his memories. And why should he have felt the need to relive the poverty and the prejudice? I knew that my mother's parents died before I was born. My father's mother had also died. When I was in my third year at medical school, suddenly, as if the information had dropped from a cloud, yet released by a secret mechanism in my self, I learned that my father's father was still alive, ninety-three years old, living in a nursing home in upper New York State, that he had lived there, in failing health, for many years. I remembered having seen him once or twice during my childhood, and then the year I went to college he disappeared out of our life, and he had been so unrelated to our way of life that I honestly never questioned

8

his disappearance; I took it for granted that Grandfather had no place in our life.

When I discovered that he was alive, I was told that he was well looked after, that he had everything he needed, including a private room, a TV, and medical attention. Even at that time of my life I did not question the glib nature of the information.

I visited Grandfather. I found him to be an old old man like a Russian patriarch (he had been born in Russia), like a character strayed out of *War and Peace* as Pierre had strayed on the battlefield. I had a dim memory of having visited him before, of saying 'Hello Grandfather,' and of being banished then to wait in the car.

He had no disease except the frailty of old age. He needed a nurse to clean him. He wore a permanent gentle smile, with an air of listening and waiting, which is perhaps all one can do at that age, in that state of frailty. When I saw him it was fall and his room was filled with leaf-light from the trees outside his window, and his skin was tinged with gold, and I had a memory of the childhood story of the Happy Prince who had been flaked with gold and who gave it away, flake by flake, to keep others warm, until only his heart was left, and this too was taken, by a bird, a brightly coloured spring bird like a scarlet tanager, a robin, a red cardinal that was in the room all the time, disguised in the leaf-light. But the Happy Prince had been young, and reckless.

My fantasy surprised me. I remember thinking that my grandfather had no gold to give away, that he was keeping his yellow skin. When I returned home I found the rest of the family reluctant to talk about Grandfather.

'How is he?'

'He's doing nicely. He's failing but he seems happy.'

Everyone sighed, a sound like the faint whirr made by the

garbage disposal unit when it comes to rest after doing its work.

'Dear dear Grandfather. Dear dear Grandfather.'

One weekend when I was in my fifth year at medical school I came home to find that the garbage unit, so to speak, had failed. The nursing home where Grandfather was living was closing down and had asked that he be removed as soon as possible. Already my parents had made inquiries and had found no vacancies in other nursing homes in the area. I thought naively, There's no problem. Grandfather hasn't more than a few years to live. He can live here at home. Ben and I are grown up, Mother isn't so busy she won't be able to cope. He can die here at home. He can live and die here.

Thinking of the world 'die', of the fact of death so clearly, I had the feeling that I had suddenly burned my lips with acid.

I persisted in my thought that Grandfather could die at home. By this time I'd had experience with dying patients at the hospital and I was becoming interested in dying and death and resenting the way I had been deprived of experience of death almost as I would have resented being deprived of love. I was amazed that both I and my family considered and dismissed the possibility of Grandfather's coming to live with us.

'We'd like to have him here but it's out of the question.'

Why did I not argue?

Grandfather was transferred to a nursing home near the border of Canada and in a dreamlike journey I went to visit him through blue snowlight in the darkest month of winter, and where before his room had been bathed in leaf-light, now it was filled with a nightmarish glow as if a television set had been swtched on in the sky, beaming its programme toward the earth, an illusion which Grandfather sustained in the way his eyes searched restlessly, following the apparent movement of the images. He did not recognise me. As I was leaving he looked directly at me.

'Do I know you?' he asked. 'Are your parents living?'

Shortly after that visit we heard that he was 'happy and settled' and six weeks later he died, presumably happy and settled.

At the beginning of the next academic year I switched my studies from embryology to death.

2

My family was proud of my decision to study medicine. There were times when my experience of it eroded my dreams so deeply that I thought of abandoning my studies. The idea of paying for the right to enjoy good health has always been abhorrent to me and to other doctors I know who would sometimes advise their poorer patients in the cities to collapse in the streets rather than attend the crowded emergency room of the hospital, as a street collapse helped to bypass the financial formalities of admission. Also, those who studied medicine were not granted qualifications for instant sainthood as I had dreamed they (and I) would be. Nevertheless it was good, I felt, to have so many hopes of personal satisfaction from my work.

There was one summer, for instance, which I spent in Peru studying the growth patterns of Peruvian slum children. It was a happy summer for me. I felt close to my family. I was at the age when a young man, waking one morning with awareness of his childhood, is at last able to separate himself from it, and it was after that summer in Peru that I began to remember and imagine my own childhood, my father's, his father's, and I became haunted by the thought of the grandfather who had been dropped like a piece of garbage from our lives. Studying the growth patterns of others I experienced concentrated growth in myself, compelled as I was then, to think about poverty and disease, of my childhood, my relatives, my military call-up which was still deferred, the possibility of service in Vietnam, and, underlying all, of death which the economy and urgency of living had abbreviated in my studies to D.

I thought of D. yet I tried to evade it by studying embryology.

The following summer I collected abortion brains from Sweden.

'Anything to declare?' the Customs Inspector asked on my return.

'Abortion brains packed in dry ice.'

The Inspector's look of shock was fleeting. 'We all have to make a living, I suppose.' He did not open the container.

That final semester, before Grandfather died, I spent all my time with the brains and with my dog Sally who had survived almost every medical and surgical treatment including the removal of one eye. I brought her to live with me in my apartment after I performed a gall bladder operation on her and when I could not face making her available for a post-mortem. I saw few people that semester. I worked long hours, going to the hospital each day through the tunnel leading from the students' apartments, and so there were weeks when I saw no sunlight or daylight and my hands became hospital hands touching sick flesh and white cloth and my face became just one of the many that I passed in corridors or met in rooms. I saw myself and others as a pair of tired eyes attached to skin attached to a white-coated body, and if I caught a glimpse of the city it was a dream city like those of cloud seen from the windows of aircraft.

I learned much about D. from the foetus brains. It is hard to put into words what I learned. The so-called death status of human beings is as subtle in influence as the classical race distinctions of their lives, death status being acceptable but unremarkable if the person lived the allotted three score years and ten, while a 'satisfactory' death would imply—as in an examination rating— a certain disappointment of expectations, supposing that death were rated, as it often is, according to the satisfaction it gives to the living. Those with the highest scores are the shocking, the tragic, the youthful—forty-three or forty-four being the boundary line of youth—for then the living are invited to invest the largest proportion of their feelings, their compassion for the dead and the family of the dead, and their gratitude for their own intact lives which grant them this generous allowance of feeling.

The death which gave me the foetus brains had little status, and could be compared to that of the forgotten aged who are not even granted the status of resentment for having lived beyond their allotted time and for having made in their dependence and frailty increasing demands upon the living. Yet my thoughts as I studied the foetus brains could centre more clearly on the nature of death as they did not suffer the life interference which persuades and changes the thoughts about the lonely aged. I began to think of death as a simple darkness and by that I do not mean the comparative ease of killing the embryo for I thought neither of agent nor instrument nor of object; I had in mind a pure personless darkness like the original void of the universe. It's a romantic notion I had; it was unscientific, as the genes and chromosomes of the embryo had already been given a generous helping of centuries of humankind and it would seem to be too late to rescue or retrieve the simplicity of nothingness—supposing that nothingness is simple, or supposing that there were indeed room for nothingness in the fullness and complexity of the life cycle.

You ask what has this to do with a foetus brain? I mean that in thinking about death I discovered a small silent area of pure darkness, a sanctuary for the dying, as the wetlands and wildernesses are sanctuaries for the fleeing wildlife. And I felt that those who had lived and were dying had as much right to find that sanctuary as the embryos which had scarcely lived had found it. I was aware that it might be my sanctuary rather than that of the slain foetus but I was a student of medicine to learn what I thought the body in all its conditions might teach me, even if it was my personal experience and dreams which prompted the subject of the lesson. The brains taught me their size and substance because I knew how to measure them scientifically. They taught me about D. because after my time in Peru I felt I was ready to use the special instruments I had devised in my heart.

You might ask why a young doctor was so ready to take time to think about death when according to natural laws and bylaws he should have been preoccupied with love and sex. Before I was twenty I had a passionate love for an older woman and when my parents learned of this they set in motion immediately the excruciating process which parents may use to force their son to forget what they think ought to be forgotten: they sent me to Europe to collect pieces of sculpture, and as with my later gathering of the foetus brains, I learned to shop outside my home, in foreign lands, for some knowledge of myself and life and death, and to bring home like a hunter the twin trophies of creation and destruction.

I had no other love until I met Lenore who gave her feeling to me as one gives a package which is accepted and, with an absence of mind, signed for. This was after Grandfather's death when I had begun working as an assistant in the Department of Death studies in New York where I had rented an apartment for the summer— a fourth-floor walk-up in a plain ugly building which I chose because I needed to live in surroundings completely different from those I had known, in my home and in my other hospital apartment where all (so I told myself) was the essence of good taste with my pre-Columbian pieces set around the room, my Indian rugs on the floor, my Ethiopian murals on the wall. I felt that I needed the inhumanity of my temporary city apartment where the tenants were looked on as part of the fittings to be removed or changed if they failed to satisfy. Sally lived with me, and Lenore visited and stayed often.

Lenore and I had arranged to marry. She was working at a clinic for sexually unfinished children and I dislike to confess that both I and my family looked on her as a prize. If I told Lenore how much I valued her I would have been insulting her, as, whether or not I realised it at the time, I gave the world 'value' no more nor less than its literal meaning. She was something I had won and in marrying her I would make my winning public. My brother Benjamin adored her tall blond beauty, her cleverness, what he called her 'style'. My mother approved of her although she was not Jewish and her father (my family did not know this) had been a Nazi official during the Second World War. Panicking at the prospect of my never marrying, my mother had lowered her ethnic sights and searched for kinship rather than for differences in our backgrounds; her principal quoted example was that we were both from families which, though not native Americans, had since become staunch Americans.

It was to my father that Lenore endeared herself. The two would flirt at the meal table with her paying him outrageously

16

exaggerated compliments which he accepted with only a pretence of disbelief. On Sunday mornings he liked to take a bath, singing as he soaped himself the tunes from the opera lessons he once learned, for he had a fine tenor voice. Then Lenore would prepare her praise for him with the skill of a cook preparing a gourmet delicacy, and present it to him when he emerged rosy and warm-eyed from the bathroom. It was his delight also to take her on a tour of the house to show her his paintings and explain them to her while she listened with interest and understanding.

'She'll be a real asset to the family,' he used to say.

I noted once again the tendency to make a material judgment of her as if she were a gilt-edged share in which I was about to invest my emotional fortune and of which the dividends were anticipated happily by every member of my family. Her undoubted value locked her within the business world of my family with the marriage contract legalising the deal. I realise that I thought more of her as a partner in my work than as a future wife.

When I tried to explain about Sally, how she had helped to ease the distress of my early experiences at the dissecting table, and how I found I could operate more readily on her in her role of familiar pet than on an unfamiliar dog, as Sally always showed her trust in me, Lenore became upset.

'I can't understand why you have been able to mutilate an animal you love while you dislike cutting open animals you have never seen. I should have thought it would work the other way. You do love Sally, don't you?'

I agreed that reason appeared to have little place in my attitude toward mutilating Sally, and that one might have thought that a loved creature would be harder to hurt than one unloved.

'Our work is a science, Talbot. You know that. You have to use clear reason. You know what the professors told us— remember our first death?'

I remembered. It was something she and I shared, perhaps even more than we ever shared love. We were students both on night call, snatching sleep at any hour we could, when word came of an emergency in the Children's Intensive Care Unit. The duty was actually Lenore's but I went as support for her. The patient, a six-year-old child, was dying of nephritis and as soon as we examined him we knew there was little we could do. His parents were at his bedside. The child clutched a small doll, mimicking upon it his own many catheterisations, talking to it now and again to reassure it. Then suddenly he kissed the doll, closed its eyes and lay it beside him with its head on the pillow. Then he died.

Lenore and I faced together the hostile grief of the parents and our own ignorance of death, and that night we sat in the common room drinking numerous cups of tea and telling each other the story of our lives. The following night, for the first time, we made love: after death there seemed to be no other place to go except to love, as a way of hiding from death and, as it happened, of hiding from ourselves. Sally was there in the room. She watched with her one eye.

3

One day I was using the streets of New York as a field for my death studies. I was sitting on a bench in the upper West Eighties among the old and derelict, and enjoying the first taste of summer sun when an elderly man with a trim triangular beard and straggly grey hair, quite long as the fashion then was, sat beside me and at once began to speak to me.

'I'm Turnlung,' he said.

I was overcome by a feeling of panic which I thought, at first, was an exaggeration of the caution that is part of any conversation with any stranger in a city street. Then I had a strange feeling that I was a child and the man speaking to me was Grandfather. As I have said before, I'm not given to excessive fantasy, or I had not been before this month-long summer, nor have I been since, and so I find it hard to explain what overcame me when Turnlung spoke to me, for I found myself, after the initial panic, repeating my name.

'I'm Talbot Edelman.'

'Turnlung.'

'You're not American?' I asked, detecting his foreign accent.

'No. A visitor. I've a room down on Thirty-fourth Street be-

19

tween Lexington and Third, among the Funeral Homes, along from the Terminal.' He meant the East Side Airlines Terminal of course yet the way he pronounced the word, the peculiar emphasis he put upon it, brought back my feeling of panic. I looked at him, at his face, his eyes; they were an old man's clouded eyes, the surface of the whites curdled, yet seeing them as they were I also saw them as clear eyes; they were clear blue, they were smiling.

'I've come to this land,' Turnlung said, 'to take a closer look at death. At my own death. I'm an old man, restless as at the commencement of a journey. In my so-called twilight pre-occupation it may be that I have chosen death instead of sex, shrouds instead of skirts.'

He glanced questioningly at me.

'I'm a writer,' he said. 'I want to investigate dying and death.'

I felt fear once more. I wondered if he knew about Grand-father, the Invisible Living Trash. Since Grandfather's death I had become obsessed with elderly men in each of whom I saw the grandfather I never knew, who was hidden from me, whom I hid from myself, my first death that was no death; and I saw myself as an old man, I was face to face with myself and I did not know how to act. My first impulse was sexual. I wanted the old men to enter me with all their baggage of history, their own past and the past of their ancestors, as if somewhere in my mind and body I kept an unstocked larder from which I was being constantly turned away in needless hunger when some act, some chance miraculously might have filled the empty shelves. I attributed much of this feeling to my having been deprived of experience of death. I wanted the old men to give me, free, *their* deaths.

I began to talk to Turnlung. I told him of my death studies.

'I hope you include your own death and mine,' he said. 'At

20

your age you should be getting your death experience through loving. That, and normal family experiences. Would you like to study my death?'

I must have looked shocked. 'Of course not,' I said. I told him, however that I was interested in his feelings about death, that I wanted to know details of his death education as I myself had had none.

'No death education? A citizen of a country of death, with no death education?'

If you read this you may laugh at me if you wish. I did not dream Turnlung. My God, I did not dream Turnlung.

Yet that night in my sleep I lay in long grass in a foreign land, and Grandfather with the sky above all to himself, all the snowclouds and stormclouds and blue belonging to him, was standing near stamping his feet in their snowboots, against the cold.

A nurse appeared. 'Everything is provided,' she said, reading from a scroll of parchment like the parchment skin of the dead. 'He has everthing he needs. A locker for his toilet and shaving gear. A closet. Television. He can potter about and talk with those of his own age who understand him. He's in good hands.' She made a gesture with her hands, as conjurers do, to prove they have drawn their materials out of thin air.

The nurse was my mother. Pinned to her uniform, on the left breast, was a garishly coloured joke button which I could not deciper. Then I noticed my father, although I did not recognise him at first for he was as old as Grandfather and he too was stamping his feet against the cold, and his voice was querulous as he complained that the sky did not belong to him, asking why did it not belong to him, hadn't he bought up the sky in all his paintings in all these years?

He carried a painting which he unwrapped, in the middle of the field, to show us. A sunny painting. Good fortune, love and life and home and country. Surprisingly, the nameplate said *Siberia*.

Father and Grandfather were talking together. My father pointed to the scene in the painting.

'What do you think of it? Do you like it?'

Grandfather began to shout. 'Do I like it? It's comfortable. They give you a locker and you're allowed a few possessions but it's a lie, a lie, a lie. Why do you pretend there's no death? This isn't the South of France, the sunny meadow. Why are you stamping your feet if not to stop icicles from forming in your blood?'

It began to snow. I watched the flakes falling through the grey-green sky onto the two old men who now talked to each other as strangers, quietly, politely.

'Are your parents living?' my father asked.

'Do I know you?' Grandfather replied.

They repeated the questions to each other. Merging with the snowfall they became faceless, they could have been anybody, even Turnlung. They became the old men, a species as ancient as the spiders of the Silurian age; the old men who precede and shadow the young through their life, who rehearse their death for them; the wicked and the wise whose active part in the drama has lapsed and who become the foolish distributors and interpreters of directions and messages; the onlookers valued for their age and their secrets, full of warnings of 'dire combustion and confused events newhatched to the woeful time', the old soldiers who, dying, were remembered as men of marble and stone, on horseback in parks and squares and marketplaces; the poor sick mad old men who wander the streets of the city; the old men who are still the creators and performers of music, painting, poetry, who, like God, still work a day's work and see that it is good; the complainers—'everything alters'—and the rememberers who look through their memory as through a telescope to magnify and make immediate the happenings that were far away and long ago; and those who may practise at last the unique art of dying and learn the secrets of death and the dead.

The snow was still falling. Now it covered the painting that lay in the grass, and soon it covered the two old men. The blinding snowlight forced me to close my eyes against the scene and the dream. I woke, thinking of Turnlung, and remembering that we had arranged to meet again.

PART TWO

THE BEES IN
THE FLOWERING
CURRANT

4

I am an old man, a traveller down Instant Street, with water in the corner of my eye and milkwhite seeing. I move my arm like a rusted reap hook to clear away the undergrowth growing me under. I am in a foreign land, in the city of the diesel sun where no one believes in crocuses yet where much emphasis is on springtime, eternal life; a city of pursuit where man plays cops and robbers with pyramidions, moon rocks, and the protein molecules of his own life. Knock on the doors and windows of the planets. Is anyone home? Is anyone alive?

I move, it is alive, kill it.

They said to me, 'Haven't you an answer, Turnlung? Most men have an answer by their seventy-fifth birthday.'

I said that to survive, from the moment we are born, we must be capable of turning against. Before birth we are against air, against breathing, yet we survive to breathe and love the air, we become turncoats—turnskins, turneyes, turnmouths, turnhearts, turnlungs. And having known life we are against death even when all messages from the country of death convince us that our final role must again be that of turncoat—turnheart, turnlung.

I have ever needed to be in advance of myself, to be able to defend myself against the onslaughts of future time. The symptoms and states of old age—physical difficulties such as failing eyesight, stiffening joints, occasional dizziness, restlessness, insomnia—the premature waking at the acknowledged death hour when the morning has scarcely begun to take shape and light is a promise which may or may not be fulfilled.

Although these were not all mine I gathered them about me in advance, as weapons, instead of recoiling from them as assailants. At the first hint of failing eyesight I phoned the Institute of the Blind to arrange for lessons in Braille. They refused me. There were enough of the blind, they told me, without trying to care for those who would steal a march on their own blindness; in effect, on their own death. When I hinted that training for both blindness and death was necessary their reply was that blindness as a landmark toward death and ultimate darkness was like a privileged club requiring qualifications for entry. As I stood in their huge old building where the vast corridors were lapped in slow measure by the groping current of deliberating footsteps and unseeing faces, I became aware of the pride of the brotherhood of blindness and I knew that a similar mystery and exclusiveness surrounded the community of the dying and the dead. I wanted to enter the community of the dying. If there were tests to be passed I knew neither the questions nor the answers. I could learn nothing, rehearse nothing. The sources of information—the dead—were inaccessible to me.

Therefore I made my voyage to this country where death appears to be more important than life, where the secrecy of death is found even in the country's government which emphasises secrecy as if they, reflecting or imposing the preoccupations of all, were returning to childhood to play at secrets in a rehearsal for the keeping of the last secret. Their vocabulary is the vocabulary of death. A traitorous agent 'crosses to the other side'. Entrance is gained by a 'password'. The dying 'pass on', their password uttered.

'He sendeth out his word and melteth them; he causeth the wind to blow and the waters to flow; he showeth his Word.'

It is a consuming mystery, the game to discover the secret, the game of trying to identify the last silence, and, hardest of all, the game of learning to accept and love the silence. I play the game as well as I know how to. I've carried out experiments with words, my mix of amino acids. I still sit each day before my typewriter. I think a fearful calamity will strike me, I sense myself growing old and feeble, an outcast among the one-third blind. Now, in this city, I see everything with a molecule of sulphur dioxide, like a pearl, as a mote in my eye.

Here, death is safely within the delusional dream dreamed by the dollar-people. Here, death has been domesticated. It is the exile at last welcomed home. The dead lie here in Funeral Homes not, as before, and as in many other lands, at the Undertaker's, the undertaker being the person paid to undertake the task of getting the dead under, out of sight and mind. At the Funeral Home the dead are welcomed by the Host. A little research among words will show that the original host was *hostis*, the enemy. Language, at least, may give up the secrets of life and death, leading us through the maze to the original Word as monster or angel, to the mournful place where we may meet Job and hear his cry,

> *How long will you vex my soul*
> *and break me in pieces with words?*

* * *

I hear them in the night, feeding. They do not stop for sleep as we do. Eating is their life. They must devour the mulberry bush. Wherever I go I hear them. Were I dead, waiting to be buried, lying in my allotted drawer in the mortuary, I should hear the silkworms eating through the ice to reach me.

How tired they are, and fat and old! They have shed their skins many times and soon when they have stripped the mulberry tree of its leaves they will stop eating and each will begin to wave its head about like an idiot, and drool golden threads of silk, using the silken adhesive to seal itself to the place it has chosen or the place that has been chosen for it. And then all day and night each silkworm will work to shroud its body in gold until one morning the filled shrouds hang in the shape of bullets or punctuation marks and all is silent.

I cannot be curious enough to inspect them or touch them; their privacy is the privacy of death. They have devoured the mulberry tree, transforming it to silk. Yet I want that silk! I want that silk so desperately that I interfere, as artists must, with the process of life and death. Taking a pair of scissors I cut through the walls of the silk shroud, shaking out the lily-pale grub onto a makeshift bed of cotton wool. The grubs are nothing, they are pure sensation; they recoil, quivering, at a touch. I bury them, wrapped in their man-made shrouds. Then taking the empty cocoon I find the end of its thread and I begin to unwind the thread, then I have an unravelled shroud that is a spool of silk, and all the freedom in the world to do with it as I please. First, I plait it. I keep it in front of me as a trophy of life and death.

Later, I uncover the buried grubs that now are a burned brown colour. There is a constant wriggling motion inside their skin. I watch as one by one pale crumpled moths emerge, rest awhile, spreading their damp useless wings, then crawl blindly to each other, the males mounting the females and beginning at once, from birth, the copulation which lasts a lifetime for the male who dies following his final thrust while the female lives only to lay her eggs like delicate stitches on a seam or small white beads upon an abacus. Then she too dies. I bury their eggs. If I unearth them in the springtime I can again watch and take part in the life and death cycle—that is if I do not ever forget where to find the leaves of the mulberry tree which gives shelter from the sun and of which the name is a phonetic accident.

Oh I did not come to this land as a joyous traveller or an April pilgrim. I have consumed many deaths in a mountainous banquet set before me. I have devoured them all until reaching my own death I achieve the miracle of metamorphosis, round and round the mulberry tree on the cold and frosty morning of language. Grief is noisy. Grief goes on all night while the rest of the world is sleeping. Grief can spin the silk that you must cut to the core, unwind, plait, removing all traces of the toil and the impossible life, love and death of the makers, before you set your golden trophy on display.

*   *   *

It is a sullen yellow-burning day in early summer. A strike has paralysed the city. Garbage may not be picked up; bodies may not be buried.

I write from a land where the Bible is written in the daily newspaper:

In the beginning he put eight white mice, four pairs into an eight and a half by eight and a half foot galvanised steel universe on the upper floor of a corrugated iron building. The mice had warmth, food, no disease, and no predators to fear. In a little more than two years there were 2200 mice. But by that time they were not mice any more. They were non-mice. Time has not yet run out for man.

It is this great leap in thinking, from mice to men, that puts frowns on the faces of some scientists.

I write from a land where the obsession is the death of all and the resurrection of all, including the people, if they can be found and distinguished among the dead and resurrected flavours, colours, fish, insects, animals, plants, seasons, images (as in the disintegrator-integrator processes of televison). I think of the words of Malraux: 'It looks like a very simple thing to see a man where there is a man, and not a camel, a horse, or spider. It is nevertheless this clear eye, this absence of madness which today passes for madness.'

I write from a land as haunted by death and guilt as the Ancient Mariner, though here the mariner is young, he is the young Marine who has recently killed. Here, no one knows whether the dice game between Death and Life-in-Death has been played, nor what stage of suffering the mariner has reached. Could it be where 'in his loneliness and fixedness he yearneth towards the journeying moon and stars'?

* * *

These are dangerous days. Lying so still, in silence. It has always been dangerous to stop.

I am tied down to my stem.

Today I, Turnlung, pulled up my roots to inspect them. Some of the nerve endings are withered; others are frozen;

none search to push open the mouth of the earth.
Have you ever noticed, waking in the morning,
the root-fibres clinging to your lips?

My green stem had a bitter taste.
My heart knocked like the stick of the blind
up and down the stone steps. Early in my life a romantic
    notion
settled on my literate fruit. I was flyblown by Shelley and
    Keats,
by the blind and the mad, and
the picture I had of old age
was that which all hold onto in the hope its value will increase.

I'm tired now. At my back I hear
the constant whirring of the airconditioner.
Soon it will be summer, mad midsummer. The daymaking sun
    treads
on the sweating people, on their carpeted heads;
the floor-walking sun, inspector of bone and its container, skin,
    suspects but cannot prove
those women in the street have lately made off with a load of
    sperm.
They have many cavities, and are full of body.

And all the time I, Turnlung, have been getting ready for my
    own great moment.
You think I will not recognise it?
You think I will fight before I start to kiss the signature of
    my speaking diploma?
I, Graduate Turnlung, wrapped in parchment skin or silk
pocketed by death, let in to the earth and the secret that

33

consumed me. I'm anybody,
anybody with age-spotted skin, my bones mountainous,
my cataract, my avalanche of blindness rushing me out to the
  oceans of night.
You think that I, Turnlung, will fight?
I am a bottle with a message in it. I will float back and forth
  in the dark for many years.
No one may find me in the first landfall.
Or the second. Or the third.
Then one day or night when those who knew me have forgotten I existed,
then someone will find me, my message will get across,
all along that ruined coast littered with language,
with see-through words, glass words, bleaching words, indestructible synthetic words
helping to complete the big fish- and people-kill.

Being born I rejoiced that I did not remain fish.
And yet, at the last, I assist in the carving and distribution of
  my treason-tempting lung;
at the last, which may be soon; almost now; how quiet it is;
it is called a legal certified hush.

Slowly from the word-throng the proud chosen come forward:
  goodbye seasons, learned like products,
goodbye earliest morning,
goodbye habits, and love that got nowhere for want of,
goodbye rhyming city, lost the nail, the shoe, the horse, the
  rider and the kingdom.

5

I, Turnlung, have experienced a succession of deaths as one experiences a succession of loves. I have been in and out of death, each time thinking I had the intelligence to profit from my experience. The first death in my life was that of animals, a death explained in a simple sentence. The cat is dead. The calf is dead. The rabbit is dead. In my country death was often the equivalent of careless litter cast by water, ice, snow, lightning, with the human victims quickly removed from the scene and the animals lying untouched as earth-hosts to the mushrooms growing up through the skulls and the buttercups blooming in the rib-cages. The paddocks with their remains of sheep and cattle and horses were like old battlefields, the land was a cemetery wilderness where cattle and sheep grew in the gardens as summer flowers, bloomed below the snowline as orchids and mountain lilies, were housed in the bones of the people as real deposits that have never been withdrawn.

The dead cat was my first death. I remember it as I remember my first love. The cat was ugly in death, its fur was matted and wet, its eyes were deep in their sockets. It lay under the flowering currant bush where honeybees swarmed about the clusters of tiny purple bell-like flowers, and for me the purple flowers and the golden bees became part of the smell and sight and sound of death, as spring became the season of death. I grieved for the cat because what had been in it had vanished. I never dreamed, as I understand it now, that the animal's death was the meeting of its presence and its absence, where before I had known each only separately. If two is richer than one, then the cat and my knowledge of it were richer in its death. I knew then only that it lay cold and stiff, that death was a shelterless time when the rain rained and soaked through, and the sun shone uncaring, and the noisy bees went on ransacking the flowers and making their honey.

Then followed my first personal human death—Grandfather's. Although he lived in our house I never felt that I knew him. He had a room of his own with a bed to sleep in. There was a place for him to eat at the table, a chair for him to sit in by the fire. He wore clothes that were spoken of as belonging to him—Grandfather's overcoat, Grandfather's boots. He walked stiffly from room to room. He walked in the garden and he sat on the wooden seat beside the clump of red dahlias. He used the bathroom. He coughed, talked, complained, and he wore rimless glasses. That was Grandfather's essence, gathered, aged, bottled, where our home was the bottle.

One night he died in his sleep. He went away and his absence remained with us. His body was put in a box shaped and coloured like a ripe acorn, and carried away and buried in his own special place in the earth, and for a time his bed and his room and his chair, the spaces he occupied about the house and in the garden were hungry for him as though each day he lived they had fed upon his presence; his clothes were hungry, too—his boots with the narrow leather laces like strips of licorice; his overcoat with the shiny brown lining, iridescent like the wing of an old starling. I knew he was dead. I listened to the conversation of the adults and I caught their acceptance of his death and their judgment of its ease or difficulty, yet I never learned to know his death as I knew the death of the uncared-for black cat. Grandfather was removed too quickly from the scene. I remember that one day seven years later I was rummaging about the house when I found a spectacle case which I opened. A pair of rimless spectacles lay upon the crushed blue velvet lining. The sight of the spectacles and the blue lining brought a sudden pain of longing, a wild grief for Grandfather, the kind of grief I felt when I watched the bees dancing about the flowering currant bush, and it seemed as if Grandfather's death, all those years, had been confined in the spectacle case and my opening it had released the death like a fume of memory. His chair, his bed, his room, his places everywhere around the house had long ago given up their habitual attachment to him, but his tenacious spectacles in their velvet-lined case still held his life and his death. By then I knew enough of memory to realise it was a bargain to have traded a dimly remembered time for a pair of spectacles in a case lined with blue crushed velvet.

I knew that the dead were confined and removed as quickly as possble and that deaths varied in importance, and although I might love an animal more than a human being, the extent of being rather than the extent of loving was what mattered when aids to memory were being planned. To place a memorial, 'Gone but Not Forgotten', above an animal would have invited ridicule whereas someone unloved might be given this wishful memorial as a right. Animals, my parents assured me, had no place in the 'kingdom'.

We had buried the cat in the garden near the flowerbed. Two

Sundays after Grandfather's funeral I saw where they had buried him. It was a place new to me; it was populated entirely by the dead. I had seen such places as we passed in the train and pointed to the rows of tombstones sharp and white as molars (at that age, getting and losing teeth, we had their image ever in our minds). Grandfather's cemetery was a gently sloping hillside overlooking the town and the sea, sunny in summer, chilly with seawind in the evenings and in the winter. For the Sunday visit we wore our best clothes (I had a new pair of braces and I had the old ones in my pocket to use as a shanghai, for I took pleasure in using shanghais, in collecting the right size of stone and in thrilling to the warning that another boy's eye could be knocked out, or my own eye, if another boy fired at me). My big sister and I carried a bunch of flowers picked from the garden—poppies, marigolds, pansies, lavender—my mother having removed the buttercups and stinking dog daisies which were not deserving enough to be included. We walked the long walk to the cemetery. We found it to be divided into small plots like the private places or 'possies' which my friends and I claimed for ourselves when in the midst of games we suddenly decided we wanted to be alone and inaccessible.

Grandfather lay buried in his possy. We put our flowers in their jamjars and stood back to see the effect. The tall tombstone, listing the dead of my father's family, had room for many more names, and already Grandfather's name had been lightly marked in, like a tentative booking for a concert. Some of the surrounding graves, cared for with housewifely grief, were like polished front rooms in their floral and marble splendour; others were overgrown with lank yellow grass and the white onion flowers which, at a distance, with the wind blowing in the wrong direction, could masquerade as snowdrops. We walked up and down the aisles of the graves inspecting the stone angels, matured with most of their bodily parts or infantile, with stone creases in the significant places. Some tombstones were broken, others were hidden by the grass and the onion flowers; wet clay mounds piled with wreaths trailing wet magenta and black and white ribbons told of fresh graves, and by then I was advanced enough in cemetery lore to know that in time Grandfather's grave would 'sink', as these would, to a level with the earth. Of the many housewifely graves some had everlasting flowers around the stone edge, like vases of flowers on a windowsill; and gravel beds like those in small new housing developments where the emphasis is on the surroundings which give the least bother, thus permitting the inhabitants to enjoy more leisure. In the entire cemetery there were perhaps four or five families who were important and rich enough to place their dead in small marble houses with elaborately carved pillars ('look at the lovely pillars,' someone said, and I thought they meant pillows), and with cypress trees bordering what would be the 'front path' from the street.

'Cypress trees,' Mother said. They were unlike any trees we had seen before; with their tightly furled secretive dark foliage they were less trees than grim shadows growing in their own light, independent of the sun.

Every Sunday from that day we took flowers to Grandfather's grave. I remember feeling that our family now had a purpose in life—to care for the dead. I sensed that my grandmother whose death I did not remember had been subjected to the same ritual until the persistence of grief and memory failed, and even within a few Sundays after Grandfather's death I could feel its force draining away. Although we enjoyed the visit to the cemetery, for we thought of it as a happy peaceful place, few buildings and all sky, and putting flowers

on the graves was like tucking someone up in bed, we knew
that it was strictly temporary, that we had only a brief loan
of the dead. In time we no longer visited the grave. I forgot
about it. Everyone seemed to forget. Death was once again
back where it belonged—in the columns of the newspapers,
in history books, in the gossip of the neighbours over the back
fences, the rumours of accidents and sickness in the white stone
hospital on the hill. It was a relief to get rid of death. There
was a wild feeling of freedom as at the departure of an
unwelcome guest after a prolonged exhausting visit when the
relationship was about to become finally that of host and
parasite.

6

Each of us inherits for use in our death education a supply of private and public deaths as numerous and memorable as our supply of loves. If I search my own death store I find a collection representative of the kind most people have. In a country of earthquake and volcanic activity we naturally take imaginative possession of recent and remote upheavals from everywhere. I hold the Vesuvius eruptions as if I had lived through them. I see the sterilised pumice dead in all their poses of living and loving and I remember the childhood rumours that one could walk among the dead in Pompeii and break off pieces of people to take home as souvenirs (I did not realise that this is always the pastime of tourists), that a woman could scrub herself in her bath with a man's pumice testicles. At school, in history, I learned of the lava burial of my country's Pink and White Terraces which few in my generation had seen but which everyone spoke of with wonder and a sense of loss. In the same way I acquired earthquake deaths, the shipwrecked, the dead of many wars, of all wars, including the Crusades where the soldiers, knowing that death is 'heavier than the heaviness of all things', dressed themselves in iron mail to die.

Then, with the invention of radio and television we were suddenly given more deaths than we could cope with, and now we not only inherited them, we are invited to witness them. Where the written word allows us to siphon off small doses of death, the image in the moving picture does not even wait to invite us, it abducts us to the scene with the result that we have a collection of unformed, ill-matured, ungrieved-over deaths in our storehouse and a scarcity of feelings to match them. The periods of grief, of mourning, are curtailed or lost, the death itself has no silence in which to become real; often our supply of feeling ceases, and aware of our poverty, while the deaths continue, we begin to hate; having no other feeling left to give to the demanding deaths we give ourselves, we become death as surely as those who love become the beloved, 'by just exchange one for another given'.

So I have shared these deaths by volcano, tidal wave, shipwreck, cyclone, all those acts described in steamship and air tickets as Acts of God, and many including genocide which are acts of man. The total confuses and sickens. We take out the dregs of feeling and gum them dutifully to the appropriate deaths, as if we were fixing stamps in a stamp collection, and we begin to fear that like the astronauts who walk on the moon we can do no more than record and file and exclaim, like creatures in a comic strip. It is not the birth explosion but the death explosion which threatens to bankrupt man of all that makes him human.

* * *

Two isolated masses of death are marked on my map. My death education had settled into what might be called a 'learning plateau', a levelling of the graph of shock; it was a

42

time spent on the lonely savannah under the searching sky waiting for a death to give meaning to life, for as death education is curiously expendable, so I had quickly used up past deaths. Then came a classic accident—a train crossing the main street downtown ran over Harry Sturm. Someone was near to seize the rare opportunity to tear up sheets, and according to tradition and hygienic and humane practice, Harry Sturm was 'rushed' to the hospital from which hourly bulletins were issued during the three days of his dying. Neither King nor Pope nor President could have asked for a more fully documented death. Harry Sturm. I think he was a man whom only 'others' knew, a vague identity passed from hand to hand as buckets of water are passed to put out a fire in a distant place, or those rescued from mines or floods are passed to safety; yet though everybody and nobody knew Harry Sturm, and his life may have been a distant flicker or blaze or a sanctuary for some, all shared greedily in his death. People spoke often about him. 'Harry Sturm,' they said. 'You remember his accident? Well, Harry Sturm used to say . . . Harry Sturm used to think . . .'

He became real in an unreal way like the imaginery companions which children use as the source of their most difficult daring deeds and thoughts. Harry Sturm's death also had a romantic heroic impact, as the kind of death which could strike an ordinary man with an ordinary wife and family living in an ordinary small town on the Pacific Coast. People were horrified and thrilled by the choice of target, the manner of the blow, the accuracy of it, while discussion about who or what had aimed the blow, and why, ransacked everyone's supply of trite household philosophy.

The other death I record here was planned, violent, and indirectly involved my sister who was by then married and living in another town. Those who died, all by gunshot, were Rory Flett and his parents, and their deaths cannot be separated in my mind from the place where they lived, in a long street behind a northern hill where the sun shone on one side of the street only. The Fletts lived on the side of the street where the sun never shone and where the asphalt of the footpath had a permanent wet patch of dew and frost, or rain, or water draining from the clay bank above that was overgrown with ice plant flowering in summer in a mass of purple flowers with star-spiked petals numerous as daisy petals, which all the children picked and crumpled and scattered on their way to school. They also picked the juicy stems as the juice was supposedly a cure for the warts which came and went, in and out of fashion as much as hopscotch, marbles, baseball, or the skipping game played by the little girls,

> *Poor Sally sits aweeping aweeping aweeping*
> *Poor Sally sits aweeping on a fine summer's day.*

I never saw in any other town as much ice plant as grew in our town over every clay bank and road edge. It was said to be a member of the cactus family, living in a private desert, never growing thirsty, sucking and storing its water from the secret springs of the earth. Its flowers opened in the sun, lying flat with the heart-cushion bare, and when the sun set they drew their petals tightly together like thin purple fence-palings ranged against their heart. The hawthorn grew berries to be eaten, the periwinkle and the honeysuckle had honey to be sucked in droplets, the plantain leaves were a cure for warts and burns, but where other than in the ice plant could you find a cure with a view? The children of each generation used to sit in the spongy bed of the ice plant high above the street and the people, high enough to call out insults and to escape the anger of those insulted, and all the while they'd be rubbing their skin with the juice of the ice plant.

When I think of Rory Flett I think of him standing outside his gate by the ice plant, staring. He must have been the same age as my sister but his parents seemed to be ancient, small and wrinkled, and his mother always carried more than one shopping bag, and when I think of her now I think of the little old women who live with their bundles in the great railway stations of the world, moving from station to station at dawn when the police begin their patrol; waiting in doorways until the danger is passed.

Rory had a long face, a slack dribbling mouth, and skin with a peculiar speckle, like tweed. He was knock-kneed and narrow-shouldered, facts which we children catalogued in preparation for teasing. When my sister went downtown on Friday night to look at the boys, Rory Flett would be there. Once he asked her to go to the pictures with him but she was so contemptuous of him that he never asked again, he seemed to be contented merely to follow her around, up and down the street, and to the baths where she went also to look at the boys and to swim and to be seen swimming and sunning. Rory Flett never went swimming. He stood in the spectator area being what he was—a spectator. I remember him always as walking, following and watching. He was a great watcher. If there were men working at the telegraph poles or mending the road or tar-sealing with a steamroller, if there were a house being built or demolished, a train passing, an aeroplane flying overhead, Rory Flett would be there watching. When the workers made fun of him as they often did he did not seem to mind, he would grin and giggle and shrug his narrow shoulders.

I was far from the town when I heard of his death. I thought instantly of the ice plant. I saw the Flett house with its lacy-leaved hedge in front and the high clay bank of ice plant, and the street where the sun never shone, with the runnels in the asphalt where the water drained from the bank, and the scattered lumps of clay gouged out by the children in their search of gold.

The story was that Mrs Flett grew ill enough and Mr Flett old enough to die and as they'd always sheltered Rory at home they worried about what might happen to him. There was a place in the country, set in an acre of blue-gum trees—you could see it from the train—where the 'backward' men were looked after, in a group of low wooden buildings painted the colour of a railway station, with long seats in the sitting room like the seats on a railway platform; and it was known that Mr and Mrs Flett, when Rory was younger, had inspected the place and said, passionately, 'Never, never.' We'd heard this as children and we used to play a game where, half-choking with laughter, we suddenly said loudly, 'Never, never.'

One day Mr and Mrs Flett made up their minds. Mr Flett wrote a letter to the Police Sergeant explaining his problem and what he and his wife planned to do to solve it. Then he stamped the letter and took it downtown and posted it at the Chief Post Office, for delivery the following morning. And that night Mrs Flett took many sleeping pills, and gave some to Rory and while they were asleep Mr Flett took the rifle he used for hunting rabbits and wild duck, and shot his wife, his son, and himself.

The Flett story, I hear, absorbed the whole town. There had not been such public ownership of death since Harry Sturm's accident. The town marvelled that while the ordinary life had been going on day after day, the Fletts in their house near the bank of ice plant on the side of the street where the sun never shone had been harbouring thoughts of murder and suicide. In this case the metaphor was suitable, death having become a literal harbour.

I heard that the house was eventually sold and that the new owners chopped down the front hedge and hoed out the ice plant, hiring a man for five shillings an hour to work the rotary hoe; and it was entirely the fault of the new owners, it was said, that one night in heavy rain the clay bank collapsed, carrying the side fence of the property with it, blocking the street. Why, the town asked, did not the strangers realise that the ice plant had always been necessary to the town, to save its earth from erosion?

7

I have few inherited family deaths. The grandparents withered
and dropped like fruit. Old horses were sold as cats' meat. Old
cats with croupy coughs and half-blind watery eyes were sent
to the gas works to be 'put to sleep'. As for sheep—who ever
saw an old sheep? When I was a small boy I had a hen that
grew old and was allowed to die and I found it with its white
eye shut and its feathers ruffled as if in anger, lying under the
wattle tree. Then as I grew older with more death experience,
clusters of deaths like crops or wild flowers sprang up in families
I knew and in the homes of relatives and I learned of such
things as the value of the possessions of the dead and the
unexpected fantasies and the desperate desires of the living to
retrieve an ornament, a vase, a book, a piece of furniture, and
then when they had what they wanted, their confusion and
anger at themselves for not knowing what to do with it and
perhaps for realising that they did not want it after all.

I remember an aunt who all one summer tried to get a
grandmother clock from her dead sister's estate because, as she
said, she used to sit on the hearth and look up at the dragons
painted on the clock face, and feel how peaceful the world was,

with her older brothers and sisters away at school and she not yet old enough to go, having the house and her mother and father to herself—and the dragons; they were silver, she said, with gold flames coming out of their mouths and once when her mother took down the clock to wind it she let her trace her finger over the outline of the dragons. When my aunt finally received the treasured clock she unpacked it, examined it, identifying the dragons, almost as if she had been arguing with herself over whether she had dreamed them. Then she repacked the clock and put it under her house, in the cellar, among the suitcases growing green mould and the yellowing piles of Radio Records, and she never again unpacked the clock.

Eventually she too grew old and died. I remember her old age and death. I was never fond of her, she was always too stern and disapproving, but when she was growing old I happened to live in the same small town. I had given up accountancy and I was writing and had published stories and a novel which Aunt Kate never mentioned for the content, only for what she thought the content should be. Like most relatives she was an inveterate Why-don't-you-er. A girl cousin, Grace, Aunt Kate's 'blood' niece, and I, her nephew, were the only relatives she had in the district and Grace and I shared a few chores which Aunt Kate could not manage for herself. I mowed the lawn with the hand mower, and filled the coal buckets while Grace helped Aunt Kate bathe, and made her bed, and knitted her pink and blue bedjackets in shell patterns, in a fury of accomplishment that made me liken her to someone knitting for an expected birth instead of for an expected death. When Aunt Kate was still able to walk, using her carved walking stick, I sometimes went with her to the shops where she, of another age and household, would spend fifteen minutes choosing the best meat in the butcher's or walking up and down the aisles of the draper's reaching for the materials, holding each between her finger and thumb, gently rubbing, a faraway expression in her eyes as she 'judged' the material.

Age settles finally in a particular part of the body. It claimed Aunt Kate's back and shoulders and when I visited her she talked about them and how the doctor dismissed her complaints as 'ailments of age' as if they were broken parts of an exhausted machine which it was no use inspecting, certainly not repairing or replacing. She was at an age when there was no one to listen to her and no one to think of her as important. The Minister and the 'Ladies' from the church came to her, as Grace and I did, as a duty, and all listened politely, passing the analgesic buck when she complained that the pills the doctor gave her did not ease the pain in her back and shoulders.

I too spent my time in false consolations. The question of an old people's home had arisen and I, who thought an institution to be the last place in the world for anyone to die, heard myself telling Aunt Kate of an uncle I knew on my mother's side who had spent his last days in an old people's home; how happy he had been with his own room and some of the flowers from the garden arranged in a vase on his dressing table where he had *five* drawers for his clothes. (I remembered the wonder-filled emphasis by the grownups on the number of drawers, the marvellous bounty of storage space, and how I'd been to visit Uncle Ted and expecting to have a mystery unfolded I had stealthily opened the five drawers to find that four were empty, lined with plain white paper with dark specks on it, like the paper the grocer used to wrap the bread in, while the top drawer held in one corner a small pile of clothing like a collection of clothes for a boy doll.) The properties of heaven could not have been described more enticingly by me as I talked of the old people's home. And, like heaven, the home had an unsurpassed view, rivalling (I thought but did not say) the view from the hilltop cemetery. Then when Aunt Kate spoke of dying I, who imagined I was being well educated in death, insisted she would live to be a hundred and receive a telegram from the Prime Minister.

'But I want to die,' she insisted. 'Life hasn't been the same since Uncle Dick went.'

Uncle Dick was her husband but as parents often call each other Mum and Dad, she had always called her husband Uncle, as the children closest to her were her nieces and nephews, the 'blood' relatives, of which I was not one.

I was out of town when I heard that Aunt Kate had a slight stroke and had been admitted to a private hospital for aged women, as a permanent patient. I visited her. She was in an upstairs room which she shared with another woman. She was sitting in her brand-new nightdress and her day's choice of bedjacket, dozing in front of a caged gas fire.

'What a pleasant room,' I said stupidly. 'Do you get the sun?'

The walls were patterned with small pink four-petalled flowers linked by leaves somewhat like a design on Christmas wrapping paper. Aunt Kate glanced around the room as if searching for an answer to my question. Then she peered at me.

'How like Uncle Dick you are. Oh yes, the sun comes in but I can't go out in it, I can't go down the stairs. You have just his way of putting your head.'

'Are they kind to you?'

She shrugged. 'It's as good as I can expect. I don't like the meals.'

'Do you get enough to eat?'

'Oh yes, there's enough to eat but you have to ask for it, you have to press the bell and they get annoyed with you if you ask. And my fingers can't press. I keep losing my glasses, too, and they don't like having to look for them. The tea is terrible. It's already poured when you get it. I've always liked to pour my own and to put in my own milk and sugar. I wish I had a marmite sandwich or a thin slice of ham. And they never give you soup. I always had soup at home. Barley soup. Don't tell Grace I'm saying all this, she might worry. If Uncle Dick knew,' she said with sudden severity, 'he would never let me stay here.'

There was a tray of Get Well cards on the chair beside her. I picked up one, a religious card with two lines from Aunt Kate's favourite hymn printed inside.

I need thee every hour,
every hour I need thee.

'So like Aunt Molly,' Aunt Kate said, taking the card from me. 'She always knows what to buy for people. She always buys cards full of beautiful thoughts.'

Then she turn turned eagerly to me. 'What's going on in town today? I hate not being able to go downstairs and sit in the sun and look up and down the street to see what's going on. Are there many people in town? Are the students back?'

Like many of the old people Aunt Kate spent much of her time complaining about the students while they were in town and waiting for them to return when they were on holiday.

I visited her often. I used to bring her the evening paper, and to describe to her what I had seen on my walk to thé hospital, and as my visit was always at twilight I would tell her of the twilight cats I met sitting in front of their gates or on the gate-posts in contentment and pride of ownership, for that twilight hour was the hour of the cats, when people were home from work and waiting for their evening meal and the streets were empty and quiet and the last light lingered on the fresh spring leaves and the budding forsythia; the time just before the gloom swirled about the darkening hedges and the cold night wind began to blow from the sea; when the cats of all conditions and colour announced their possession of territory in a manner that held no threat nor challenge. Sometimes, not often, they were washing themselves; other times they were dozing, but more often they merely sat in classical cat-positions, and stared, inscrutable city cats in harmony with the quiet street and the vegetation and with the sky that mirrored their slowly moon-filling eyes.

By the time my hospital visit was over they had melted into the darkness, their hour of contentment past; they were again invisibly at love and war. Aunt Kate liked me to talk of them. For many years she and Uncle Dick had a huge silver tomcat which came to be like a child to them; they photographed it, petted it, and when it died they grieved over it. Aunt Kate had a photo of it beside her photo of Uncle Dick. I had never liked the cat. Its fur was repulsively the colour of the fat on corned beef, and it would sit all day like a round of corned beef, of 'silverside', wrapped in its fat, moving only at the hint by scent or sound or sight of something to eat.

One day as soon as I saw Aunt Kate I noticed a significant change in the position of her eyes in their sockets—they had moved far back as if they were being stored away on a bony shelf. She could no longer get out of bed and sit by the fire. She lay propped on pillows, he head lolling like a baby's, a waste of saliva like old sea-foam, at the corners of her mouth.

As one does with the dying, I could see her skeleton trying to break out of her skin, coming to the surface of her life, for use, so to speak.

She asked for a marmite sandwich on white bread with the crusts cut off but when I brought it to her she did not eat it, she merely inspected if half disbelievingly, as she had inspected the dragons on the grandmother clock.

'What's it like in the street today?' she asked.

'Busy, Very busy.'

'Are the students back?'

'No, not yet. The country people are in town today, the sheep farmers and the stock agents.'

She smiled. 'I see.'

She had been brought up on a farm and she always spoke of herself as a 'country girl'.

'Did you pass my house?'

'Yes. Your lilac is out. There are snowdrops in the hospital garden.'

Aunt Kate smiled again. 'Yes, where I live, everything is so early. My daffodils must have been out and over weeks ago. My peas and beans should be ready soon.'

She spoke fretfully. 'Isn't it time I put in my tomatoes?'

'We'd like some of your lilac,' I said. 'May we have a cutting?'

At the mention of 'we' she frowned, remembering something she disapproved of, and had she been stronger she might have lectured me once again about living an unnatural life with another man. The frown always came at the end of the lecture with the remark, 'I have nothing more to say on the matter.'

'Yes, you may have a cutting. I've had the lilac six years and this is only the second time it's flowered. We get the full sun where we live.'

She never asked after Selwyn. She pretended he didn't exist.

The next time I visited Aunt Kate the nurse drew me aside. 'This is a sad time for you. She's dying, you know.'

I could not explain that I had never been fond of my aunt, that in fact I disliked her. Yet how much I admired her! I admired her determined use of the present tense when she spoke of her home, of her life there, and of Uncle Dick. 'He likes to get out in the open on a Saturday afternoon, that's why he plays football.'

I admired her insistence that the dead Uncle Dick work for his death by accompanying her through her lonely life. When I try to think what occupied her, apart from Uncle Dick and the silver tomcat, I recall that she spent time making household preserves such as green tomato chutney, rhubarb and ginger jam, and when the berries from her beloved Central Otago came into the shops, she made strawberry and raspberry jam, beside what she made from the raspberries in her own garden. It had been part of my duty that year to prune the canes. I remember also that she kept a notebook of common and uncommon stains and their removal and she used to phone the local radio station during the Woman's Hour to give advice on the removal of an obstinate stain, and sometimes to give a recipe such as her famous recipe for girdle scones.

One morning Cousin Grace phoned me to say that Aunt Kate had died and was to be buried the next day beside Uncle Dick. I did not go to the funeral. I sent a cheap form of wreath known in the trade as a 'spray'. Selwyn and I planted the two lilac bushes, one in front the other at the back of the house near the orange blossom tree. We tended them carefully and soon the leaf buds began to unfold into the heartshaped leaves which defy a writer to trespass on the territory of Walt Whitman and T. S. Eliot. About all I can say is that the Southern Hemisphere, October, not April, is the 'cruellest month breeding lilacs out of the dead land'. It is also the month of the flowering currant.

After three weeks the lilacs withered, becoming mere dry sticks in the earth, and we thought in our paranoid way that as Aunt Kate's emissaries, they too disapproved of us. Then we reminded ourselves that we were still alive while they and Aunt Kate were dead, and soon to be forgotten. We never talked of Aunt Kate after her death. Now, from the distance of age, I sometimes think of her, how she demanded that the cup be warmed for her tea and the tea infused from three to five minutes, how she had longed for a bowl of barley soup and a marmite sandwich with the crusts cut off. And I think of her pathetic desire to 'get out under the sky and look up and down the street'.

8

How clearly, from so far away, as is the privilege of the aging, I perceive the scenes of long ago, and tears come to my eyes at incidents I never thought, once, to cry about.

I remember that when I was a boy of ten—to me the strangest, most secretive, most impressionable age of boyhood—I watched in one afternoon a concentrated adhesiveness of living and dying. I was out in the street with my friends when two dogs began to copulate and instead of separating after a decent interval they stayed together, and at first we were not surprised, making bawdy remarks to one another about how they wanted to keep doing it because they liked it so much. But when they had been together about an hour and a half and were obviously struggling to separate, we stopped joking and became alarmed. A crowd had gathered. The adults among the crowd, not aware of our knowledge of these things, made stupid remarks about how hot it was and how the heat had melted the tar on the road and caused the dogs to stick together. In the background we made hee-heeing noises deploring this tiresome explanation. No one dared to say the truth— that the dogs in all their fossicking running up and down the streets and around corners and investigating the town, had found the best sticking place in each other. Why, then, we thought uneasily, could they not separate when they so obviously wanted to? They were back to back and struggling madly for release.

What a strange afternoon of adhesiveness! The time and manner of the dogs' eventual separation are buried by my pervading memory of the tedious waiting for their discomfort to be relieved, of the alarm in ourselves, the shocked reticence of the adults when they knew that we knew, and most of all by the example of another, deathly, adhesive at work at the same time, almost directly across the road, where a linesman had been repairing the electric wires. He had been busy crouched at the top of the pole for some time, when a passerby, looking up, realised that the man was unconscious. An ambulance was summoned, and rescuers, and while the beasts on one side of the road struggled to sever their loving connection, the men opposite tried to release the embrace of death. I remember seeing the man crouched over the wires all the long hot afternoon, with the wires refusing to release his convulsed fingers and body. Again and again, or so I remember, the rescuers tried and failed to release him; he was held in a death lock. I remember my sick feeling, staring up at the crouched man, listening to the anguished doom-laden conversation of the watching small crowd who could do nothing to help. I longed for the linesman to be parted from the electric wires as I longed for the two struggling dogs to be separated.

There was a feeling as if the whole world had come alive and was preparing to reach out and grasp, as the plants do in the fairy tales, and not let go of us, its prey. The dogs had had their moments of loving, the man had had his moment of dying. Why did it not end, then and there? Why need loving and dying be such a state of prolonged attachment? I felt seized by an agonised imprisoned feeling. I wanted to free myself of the dogs, the man, the electricity greedy in the wires, the tar melting on the footpath, the soft bubbles of wet paint on the gatepost, the burnished summer flies that settled and would not be brushed off (we called them 'sticky flies'), the trailing plant that grew behind the hedge and clung to our flesh and clothes, forcibly emptying its nursery of seeds into our care whenever we touched it, the bluegum nuts which dug into us when we trod, leaving their starry shape imprinted on the soles of our feet. Escape seemed impossible. Even the supposedly detached neutral sky was hot with a blue gloss like that of gummed paper. The salt sweat of our own bodies clung to our skin in drops as big as the spiders' eggs which the spiders glued to the undersides of the leaves in the hedge.

In remembering the agony of that afternoon I have forgotten how the escape was made. How distant the scene is from the cemeteries with their peaceful absence of tenacity where the hold, whatever it was, has gone. The graves are there and the names of the dead and the faintly anxious sadness of the thought, Who remembers them?

In my early life it was the cemeteries which gave me relief from the attachments of living. When I left the small town I had been brought up in and I was studying for my degree in accountancy, I used to spend much time in a nearby used cemetery sitting on the walled graves in the sun looking down over the University and dreaming my youthful dreams, and feeling the peace that flowed over the dead who were probably forgotten and certainly abandoned and had therefore earned a contained peace, a kind of lasting settlement of the vows of death which the novitiate dead do not have, as their peace is constantly violated by the probing memories of the living.

Who said it is sad to be forgotten? it is good to be unself-conscious with the grass and the onion flowers and the wild rambler roses. It is good no longer to be or to know, to have removed even the attachment of the memory of others.

These boarding houses of the dead which have given me a haven in life by providing me with urgent separation from the living are now a material embarrassment with their corpses and tombstones. There is no place now for the dead, or for the living to learn what the dead may teach them. The dead must be freeze-dried, reduced, concentrated like emergency rations, and when you memory needs to use them it must add the reconstituting ingredient which, formerly, the cemeteries provided in their peaceful laboratories.

* * *

I have long known that the living dead like stones in their secrecy and silence are the most effective absorbers and receivers of rain, sun, words, blows; and in their own way they grow a new attached life, like moss; and it is of no matter that they are not in places where the sun will shine on them and warm them, and other living creatures, such as lizards, make use of them; they do very well in the dark damp places where death is. How could they not be said to be doing well when moss is green and green is life?

* * *

Soon I will meet and talk again with Talbot Edelman. We shall talk about death, about our personal death-history. I shall not write here of Selwyn's death or of the death of my parents, for a catalogue of deaths is not my intention. I would like, however, to tell, with some licence, of two literary deaths which were described to me by a friend, a headmistress in a northern school.

9

You may be interested (she said) in the effect which a literary upbringing may have upon death and bereavement.

My first personal experience of human death happened when I was twelve years old and my sister, four years older and apparently in good health, died suddenly, giving me the opportunity to take part without restraint in the ritual of a 'death in the family', and at the same time to learn of the loneliness of a permanent absence in the family. During the weeks following the death the word 'loss' was used in letters of sympathy and in speech and I learned the heart-distinguishing difference between this loss and those reported in the advertisement columns of the newspaper under Lost and Found, which presupposed an eventual finding if one searched far and wide enough. There was an element of searching in the passive waiting for my sister to reappear and there was also a certain kind of finding which could never have been the result of a newspaper advertisement for her life. At night I listened and listened until I learned that there was nothing to listen for, that what I hoped to hear had been receding farther into soundlessness.

This death gave me and my two sisters a feeling of importance, of newness and goodness. We bathed and were baptised in everyone's sympathy. We acquired the prestige of being in a family where someone had 'died young', a 'blossom plucked before her time', a life full of promise 'cut off tragically'. These cliches guarded the entrance to the literary nature of my sister's death. In the midst of the confusion of loss and grief and change of status (my sister was raised from a laughing devil who could lie and cheat, torture with pinches and back thumps, to a heavenly angel who could have harmed no one), of departures without return, I took the path of escape already well-worn in my life—the path to the literary death, my swift transport being a poetry anthology, *Mount Helicon*, required reading for that year at High School.

I discovered that by reading the poems I could put my dead sister where she belonged, that is, wherever I and the poets chose to put her, that I need not find words for her death, as others had found the words for me, to feed and expand my rather thin dull grief to an impressive maturity. Three poems spoke so directly to me that I was convinced they had been written for me and I was filled with admiration for the poets who knew yet could never have known my life. Browning's *Evelyn Hope* made an immediate statement of fact.

Beautiful Evelyn Hope is dead!
Sit and watch by her side an hour.
That was her bookshelf, this her bed;
She plucked that piece of geranium flower,
Beginning to die too, in the glass....

One line of the poem gave her exact age: 'Sixteen years old when she died!'

Although the name and the setting had been changed it was clear that the poet knew every detail, and I felt that my sister would have relished the imaginative generosity which gave her a bed of her own to sleep in when she had always shared, a bookshelf of her own in a house where there was one bookshelf known by its definite article, *the* bookshelf, while the piece of geranium in the glass by her bed would have appealed to her as a romantic touch, for we knew and loved geraniums with their confident pose, their energy of being and their strong pure scent and colour. Not all the poem was devoted to my sister. There were references to the writer.

> *I have lived, I shall say, so much since then,*
> *Given up myself so many times,...*
> *Ransacked the ages, spoiled the climes...*

I had learned that 'giving up oneself' and 'surrendering' were not always confined to criminals and police, bandits and sheriffs, the sensitive way in which the teacher hurried over passages about 'surrendering' and 'giving up oneself' having given me a clue to the meaning. Again, my sister would have rejoiced to know that after her furtive reading of *True Confessions* and *True Romances* and the brief heartthrobs caused by the high school boys, she had at last been given a bounty of love with one who had 'ransacked the ages, spoiled the climes'.

In the next poem, Poe's *Annabel Lee*, although the name and the setting were changed it was again clear that the poet knew intimately our small seaside town where the roar and the hush of the sea sounded day and night in our ears, and it needed little adjustment of imagination, which is no use unless it is adjustable, to think of our town as the poet described it, 'a kingdom by the sea'.

> *It was many and many a year ago,*
> *In a kingdom by the sea,*
> *That a maiden there lived whom you may know*
> *By the name of Annabel Lee.*

Other lines revealed the truth of our lives. 'The angels, not half so happy in heaven,/Went envying her and me—'
Yes, I thought, that might have been so.
The mysterious reference to a 'highborn kinsman' who

> *. . . shut her up in a sepulchre*
> *In her tomb by the sounding sea*

would have appealed, I knew, to my sister's interest in the supernatural, while the 'many and many a year ago' brought to recent grief the balm of infinite distance.

With death and burial having been taken care of by the obliging poets I was able to use the incomparable facilities for grief and mourning given by Walt Whitman in the extract from *Leaves of Grass.*

> *Once, Paumanok, when the lilac-scent was in the air and*
> *the fifth-month grass was growing. . . .*

I relived through the mockingbird my loss and mourning, from the day when the bird 'crouched not upon the nest' to its gradual abandoning of home and its final exhaustion.

For years I spent these literary riches of my sister's death. I pitied those whose death education had not begun and those who did not know the advantages of a literary death; and becoming so used to living on the proceeds of this one death, never dreaming my store would be depleted, I was shocked to find, ten years later, when another sister died, that after so wasteful a poetic spending I was now faced with literary poverty. Annabel Lee, the Lost Mate, Beautiful Evelyn Hope had made a contract, as it were, with my elder sister's death. I found this contract could not be revoked. I found I had little to give the new hungry death. I had only one story, in all its sordid detail—that of the *Gentleman from San Francisco* who sets out on a long-awaited voyage around the world, only to die within sight of Italy and to be transported home in a coffin in the hold of the ship while his wife travels alone in their stateroom. No romantic sepulchres, no mermaids, no pieces of geranium flower beginning to die in the glass, nor envying angels, and no sheltering within the grief of the mockingbird,

O heart, O throbbing heart, I am very sick and sorrowful.

My sister, Joy, and I, earning the first wages of our adult life, were to pay for our mother's first long-awaited holiday for many years, with her family in her home town two hundred miles north. Joy and my mother were to travel north by train while my youngest sister, Helen, and I stayed home.

It was late summer. The weather was perfect. Everything in the world shone with sunlight—the pine needles in the plantation quivered with light, shaking off the excess in showers of needle sparks; a gloss lay on the silver poplars, the lombardy poplars, in the grass, the sky, the birds' feathers. The wire netting in the fowl run sparkled; while the leghorns appeared to be wearing new white satin slimfit cutaway coats as they pecked at the hard-baked earth.

It was the beginning of an important year. Helen was in her first year at University, absorbed in poetry (*Epipsychidion*) and music (*Sonata* and *Symphony Pathetique*). Joy had given up teaching after a year and was thinking of applying to the Town Council for a job as a clerk which none of us had dreamed of being, as our lives were controlled not only by the literary death but by the literary life. Clerks, according to the poets we read (starting with Chaucer), were poor, pale, often tubercular. (In our home it was a virtue, somehow thought to be a matter of choice, to have 'rosy' cheeks, and in the days before our chests became breasts, to have 'fine little chests'. In the world of the poets clerks occupied their working day in dreaming of sailing to the Spanish Main or the Golden Gate, and repeating nautical terms such as 'capstan', 'bulkhead', 'port' and 'starboard'.

I also had been teaching and during the holidays I had planned to do housework. I had put an advertisement in the local newspaper, signing myself 'Educated', and I was dealing with a number of replies ('Dear Educated') which chilled me with their unadorned reality. I spoke on the phone to some who had written and I was further chilled when I heard their hard experienced voices.

In the midst of this vocational turmoil our father went back and forth to his work each day with his lunch of onion sandwiches and salmon and shrimp and his stoppered bottle of milk and the jar of sugar for his tea. He was 'shunting' at the railway yards and therefore spent all day by the Engine Sheds and the Turntable, and sometimes I brought him a hot meat pie for lunch and the small vent in the top of the pastry would be steaming and the brown paper bag would be warm and grease-stained when I gave it to him. He came home tired, the lines on his face creased with soot and coaldust, his blueys stained with coal and oil, and there'd be masses of oil-soaked cotton waste hanging from his bluey pockets. He would go into the garden and empty the crusts from his lunch tin, and peg his hastily washed blue-bordered hand towel on the rope clothesline, then he would come inside, his knees bent because he was too tired and stiff to straighten them, and he'd sit in his chair with his cup of tea on the table in front of him, spooning the sugar and stirring the twenty stirs that always made his etiquette-loving sister who had married into the family of a mayor give up hope of his social desirability.

There were as usual several cats around our house that summer. Big Puss, the great-great-great-grandmother and one each of her grandchildren who were then grandparents themselves. All were black with mixed lengths of fur, and with literary names such as Fyodor, Myshkin, Blanquette. They roamed the hills, lay sensuously in the sun, mated in the hedge, the orchard and the pine plantation, and gave birth to their kittens in the empty broken-down pigsty; choosing one from each litter to present at the house. We had lately received Matilda ('who told lies for fun and perished miserably'), a scrawny black kitten with green eyes and a whining meow which said too early in her life that no one understood her and that she may have glimpsed something nasty in the pigsty. She complained day and night. The other cats attacked her and she would sit, lonely, on top of the gatepost at the foot of the hill, near the orchard, gazing at a spot in the grass where she had once seen a fieldmouse.

In this atmosphere my mother and Joy prepared for their holiday. Joy bought a pattern and some dress material and sewed a 'summer suit' and a 'sunsuit' which were fashionable then. Ever since we had learned by chance that life might not be worth living without a summer suit and a sunsuit we had been trying to make them, often unsuccessfully either because our energy wore out ot because something irremediable happened to the neck-binding or the sleeve-fitting; or the darts puckered; or the hem dipped. Joy's summer suit, to go with her blond hair, was a success. Mother bought herself a blue silk floral dress with a navy blue straw hat to match. And at last, with the summer wardrobe and the travel arrangements completed, Mother and Joy set out on their train journey north, and we heard by phone late that evening that they had arrived.

'After all these years,' Mother said.

Satisfied, we put down the phone. In our reading, the literary life that paralleled our 'real' life, departures were not always blessed with arrival, and more often than not, the longed-for journeys remained dreams, with the clerk who dreamed of 'sailing to the Golden Gate' getting no further than his office.

> He is perched upon a high stool in London.
> The Golden Gate is very far away.

And there were others, with their unattainable Cathays and Carcassonnes.

And then, of course, there was the *Gentleman from San Francisco*.

About fifteen hours after that phone call we received another, from my mother's sister, Aunty Joy. Our telephone was old-fashioned, the kind the grocer and the butcher had, which we associated with giving and taking orders for bread and flour and meat. When the receiver was moved suddenly, and often in the midst of a conversation, the telephone would start an independent ringing, and then it would make droning noises like distant bombers, and crackling noises like a fire being started, and there would be thin faraway voices of other people having other conversations, giving news with Ohs and Ahs and I Say, and much inaudible detail. Aunty Joy's voice struggled through these interferences and at last sounded clear, and near, as she gave her news.

Our sister Joy, sunning herself on the beach (in her sunsuit!) had collapsed and died.

That was the news. There was no way of embellishing it or softening it or denying it or disbelieving it. It was just the news. Joy was dead. There was to be an inquest. After the inquest Mother would return home the following morning after travelling all night. My sister Joy would be on the train, in her coffin. They had phoned my father at work; he would make funeral arrangements.

The story of the *Gentleman from San Francisco* came to my mind. The longed-for journey, the arrival, the soul-sickening inconceivable return home.

By that afternoon the whole town knew of Joy's sudden death. The Lady Principal of the School came to visit us before we had time to clear away the telltale remnants of ourselves and our home life, and she sat in the small sooty kitchen speaking her words of sympathy, and giving us the first unexpected victory granted by Joy's death: we saw that our inhuman Lady Principal could be broken down into human molecules. Her visit was short. She left us tearful, waiting for our father to come home, and wondering how we could face him, for we knew that death is a time of apprehensive 'facing' of person and person when there's a calculation of how much love and grief it would be best to display, and a lightning reading of faces to try to compute the exact balance.

Fortunately, there was no need for calculated 'facing'. When Father came home we all sat in the kitchen and cried. Then Father went out to weed the dahlia bed and pour boiling water on the earwigs. Helen and I went to the suddenly hallowed bedroom to look at Joy's belongings strewn everywhere: scraps of sewing, unfinished hems and 'difficult' sleeves; collars abandoned on the dressing table, like half-prepared lace delicacies; lapels that had refused to stiffen, summer shoes cracked with layers of whiting; books; a collection of grasses and weeds which crackled in their dryness as we turned the pages—shepherd's purse, fat hen, rye grass, cutty grass, barley grass, feathery grass, twitch; a school workbook with drawings of faces and random remarks made on the prepared lessons; a jar of face cream; lipstick, powder, tweezers, all the aids to Joy's philosophy, 'Beauty must bear pain'. Everything was now memorable.

'She was hopeless at sewing collars,' Helen said, looking with reverence at the pile of spoiled collars.

'She stole that face cream from me,' I said.

We burst into tears.

We glanced at the pages of a letter strewn on the unmade bed.

'To the Town Clerk. Dear Sir, I wish to apply for the position advertised ...'

Other pages were addressed to a penfriend who had suddenly become warm and sent his photo and his love. 'Dear Albert. Albert dear. Dearest Albert. Darling Albert. My dear Albert...' Each page had the same clever first sentence with words crossed out, inserted, substituted. We knew Joy's diary was under her mattress and it was understood that we would not read it until everything was 'over'.

All that day we kept returning to her room to inspect her 'things'. I went to the front bedroom and opened the box on my mother's dressing table, which held newspaper cuttings of our names in school prize lists, a picture of the first flying boat, a recipe for Date Pudding, Very Special, and the newspaper reports of the inquest after my elder sister's death. The newsprint had aged to match the aging of the news; it seemed like a relic from a newspaper of last century. I reread the details which I knew by heart—the memories which the prompting of the coroner had forced into the minds of the spectators—'Yes, she looked pale that day. I heard her say she felt tired.'

It was all so distant now. Beautiful Evelyn Hope, Annabel Lee.

> *in her sepulchre there by the sea,*
> *in her tomb by the sounding sea,*

the lilac scent in the air and the 'fifth-month grass' growing—all had made a paradise, a literary haven of that early death. It was fearful, now, to be cast out of paradise with only the depressing story of the *Gentleman from San Francisco* to use for comfort, with my sister in her anxiety over her summer suit and her sunsuit seeming to be as much a figure of fun as the Gentleman from San Francisco with his toothpaste and toilet paper. My mother and my dead sister were parodying the story. My sister would be travelling in a lead coffin in the goods van of the train, with the mail bags, the holiday suitcases, cages of squawking hens and, perhaps, a sheep dog.

'She's coming in a lead coffin to stop her from smelling,' Helen said, in a kind of nursery-rhyme rhythm which recalled the end of the *Old Woman Who Lived in a Shoe*.

> *She went to the village to buy them a coffin*
> *And when she came back she found them aloffin'*.

72

Late that same afternoon my father, after polishing his shoes, for he never went anywhere without polishing his shoes, set off downtown to be seen and sympathised with, dealing with the news in his own way by being sociable, meeting his friends, and talking of 'old times'; and as his only hope at that time of day was to see his friends in the street he stood talking on the street corner, using it as the religious groups used it on Friday evenings as a place to 'save' and be 'saved'. When he came home bringing the evening paper, he had lost some of his panic.

'I saw Jimmy Woodall downtown,' he said.

And such was the intensity of our grief, running softly and secretly inside us, that it seemed as if he spoke like one of the pure in heart who had had the promise made to him fulfilled: *Blest are the pure in heart for they shall see God.*

'Jimmy Woodall? You saw Jimmy Woodall?' We spoke the name with reverence.

That night we sat around the big six-valve radio while Father twiddled the knobs, trying to get 'overseas', and then gave up, and we listened to a detective play, *Inspector Scott of Scotland Yard, The Case of the Nabob of Blackmere.* We listened until the murderer was caught and the last ritualistic sentence uttered: 'Take him away.'

We set the alarm clock for five the next morning and we woke in the night-cold, peering out of the window at the mist and dew-covered grass where here and there a circular cloud of an early mushroom appeared to float. The railway station was cold too, facing the sea barely twenty yards away with no trains at that hour to act as windbreak. Snowcoloured seagulls swooped above the platform or perched on the rusted rails of the old sidings, pecking at the gravel and the weathered grey wooden sleepers. Soon the train came rattling in. It was a 'slow' train, a goods train with trucks of sheep and other livestock, and one passenger carriage and light goods van. We had to leave the platform and walk on the gravel past the water tower and the signal box to greet our mother who was sitting looking out for us, resting her elbow on the sooty windowsill. She wore her blue silk floral dress and navy blue straw hat to match, and her return so soon, in the clothes she set out in, seemed to be a ghastly mistake made by the railways. She was the only passenger on the train. As we caught sight of her and waited for her, the sinister fact of the death returned to us. Mother climbed awkwardly from the high carriage. She was indisputably alone. No one came down quickly after her with the luggage. There was no conversation and laughter about how wonderful the holiday had been and how good it was to be home.

My father kissed her. Helen and I stood apart, looking furtively about us, like plotters, trying not to glance at the goods van. We finally looked directly at the van. Mother saw us.

'We won't be able to see her in her coffin,' she said.

Again I heard in my mind the nursery rhyme refrain,

She went to the village to buy them a coffin
And when she came back she found them aloffin'.

The undertaker who had also met the train was supervising the removal of the coffin, waiting while the hens and ducks and dogs were unloaded on to the platform. The barking and squawking and quacking disturbed the sheep and cattle in the trucks; they began mooing and bleating and we could identify the beaded trill-like bleatings of the lambs, and the calves too, mooing in the uncontrolled way they have when there is nothing to answer them. My sister in her coffin was put into the hearse to the accompaniment of an animal chorus, and as I watched and listened, I felt that I was being released from the tyrannical comparison with the story of the Gentleman from San Francisco, that Joy's death was being dislodged from the literary world and housed, with the animal cries, among the first earliest deaths I knew before I was enticed into the concealments of literature, among the animal deaths that concealed nothing, that continued naturally beyond the act of dying through the cycle of putrefaction, maggots, sculptured weathered bone, to fresh grass and yellow buttercups.

My sister was buried the next day. Only the family and the weather attended her funeral. Noticeably absent were Annabel Lee, Evelyn Hope, one mockingbird, and one Gentleman from San Francisco.

PART THREE

DOWN INSTANT STREET, JEWELS, AND THE FINISHING TOUCH

10

The hospital deaths I had known during my medical student career were marvels of cleanliness, concealments and dispatch. In the one automobile accident I had seen, the bodies and the wrecked car were removed at once and the lake of blood and oil erased so swiftly that unless I were to disbelieve what I had seen I was tempted to label it an instant Accident, a packaged deal like cornflakes, with the rescuers included in the bottom of the pack. My experience of 'field' deaths in New York was different. One day, not long after I met Turnlung, I walked by Grand Central Station, just under the bridge, and there, lying collapsed, was one of the derelict people, familiar sights in the city with their tattered clothes, their wild haunted eyes, blue-grey unshaven faces with drops of saliva like street-dew fallen overnight around their mouths. I was shocked to realise that the man lying on the sidewalk did not qualify for inclusion in my satisfying dream of other deaths and their characteristically instant disposal. I could not say,

> I saw a man upon the stair.
> I looked again, he wasn't there.

This death was a prolonged persisting death. It aroused hostility, guilt, resentment. The man was groaning, trying to get his breath, lying in the middle of the sidewalk, while the people walking past looked at him, frowned, looked away, and walked around him and hurried on, as if they were players in a game where dice are thrown to determine the number of unobstructed moves until an obstacle appears and the appropriate directions are given: Move around object lying on sidewalk. The exaggerated stepping motion of the passersby increased the illusion of its all being a game. I wanted, as a medical graduate, to feel impelled to act, either by examining the man or by calling the police or an ambulance, but I was shocked to find myself bound by the prevailing mood of the street: Let him die. He's probably shamming. He's a junkie. Let him die.

Through about seven minutes of paralysis of my body, my mind provided as through a dispenser activated by the dying man, images of the warmth and comfort of my Long Island home. I saw, in particular, the bathroom. I felt the soothing touch of the hot water, the softness of the blue-furred toilet seat, the pleasurable texture of the big towels on the heated towel rack, and though I tried, with the dying man in front of me, to concentrate on his plight and his need for help, I found I could not concentrate; my mind groped about in search of all the known means of the instant disposal I was used to.

After ten minutes the man stopped groaning. He appeared to be dead. I had done nothing to help him. A man walking his dog came by and he too would have walked on had not the dog chosen that spot to shit in. Fastidiously steering it toward the curb the man took out of a large plastic bag a smaller plastic bag and a long-handled scoop and while the dog was crouched about his business the man held the scoop in readiness, once or twice swinging it as he turned to look in horror at the corpse, as if he would have shovelled it, also, into the plastic bag. He prodded the dog to hurry. The stench familiar in New York streets rose from the curb like the smell of an instantly blossoming flower in some hideous marshland where all were trapped. The dog's mess gave off a small spiral of steam. The man retrieved the treasure, replaced his scoop, tugged at the dog's leash, and hurried away.

The spell was broken. I looked about me for a telephone or a patrol car. A siren screamed. The apparent death had already been reported. An ambulance arrived and two men carrying a stretcher scooped up the body, put it in the ambulance, closed the door, and with the siren wailing the ambulance sped along Forty-second Street. Those who had witnessed the death and had been mesmerised by it went on their way, at first still circling the empty spot where the man had lain. Then when someone unknowingly, boldly, walked through the invisible resistance, the ordinary life of the street was restored and I found again my ordinary humanity and I remembered the oath which I had taken, to care for the sick, 'to care and comfort always'.

I went home to my fourth floor walk-up and by the enticing food smell on the landing I knew that Lenore had come to cook a meal and to stay overnight. I wanted to be alone. My mind was too full of the street death to give much thought to either Lenore or to Sally who followed me, whimpering, around the apartment. I could see that Lenore was preoccupied with her day's work where she'd been interviewing parents of children with ambiguous sex identity and I felt envy of her working day set beside my one unsatisfactory death which I thought of less as a death than as an example of my failure as a human being, and the depressing realisation it brought that increasingly all I seemed to be able to learn from the dying was the confirmation of the failures of the living. There was little way of following up the street deaths, by interviewing relatives. In the hospitals I had painstakingly interviewed the families and cynically noted that the feelings they claimed to have were often presented on demand to fit the conventional pattern. Under stress, however, the truth often came out, the truth being the relief that those whose death had been longed for had died at last. 'It's like a clean sweep, doctor,' one man told me on the death of his parents, a week apart. 'I feel as if I've been reborn. I feel as if, after all these years, I've been given a licence to live.'

It was easier for him to admit the truth because his parents had had a satisfactory full life, their 'share', so to speak, and thus he was not haunted by the thought that he, personally, had stolen life that belonged rightly to the dead.

With these preoccupations in my mind, and with Lenore's musings on her own day's work, our evening was dull and silent and separate, and even our lovemaking was as though translated from the original, and in the dreamy aftermath when usually we would dredge the most personal thoughts from each other, we talked in a matter-of-fact way about our work, she of her patients, I of the dying man outside Grand Central Station. Then, realising that I had neglected Sally in not giving her an evening walk, I humiliated Lenore by getting out of bed and dressing and taking Sally downstairs. Lenore pretended to be asleep, I know, as we went out of the apartment.

Sally and I dawdled along. She had not been able to walk quickly or to run since I broke and reset the two hind legs. At the corner of Park Avenue we stopped. A man, his head bleeding, was staggering toward us. A dog on a leash trailed behind him.

'I've been shot,' he said. 'I've been robbed. Help me.'

As if this were part of an act of atonement for my behaviour earlier in the day and almost as if the man had been ordered to appear so that I should carry out by act of atonement, I took him and propped him up against the stone wall of an apartment building where, I noticed, the first floor was occupied by doctors and dentists, and seeing a light in one of the rooms I rang the bell and spoke through the entry phone. Again, the scene had been prepared for me.

'Emergency. A man shot. Fetch the doctor.'

A calm rehearsed voice said, 'Surely.'

I saw a curtain pulled aside as someone peered out through the grille. He could not help seeing the wounded man as the light from the room shone directly on him.

At that moment a police car stopped and a policeman got out and came toward me, his hand ready on his gun. I showed him my equivalent of an ID card. He studied it, and I was certain he was appraising me as a typical American citizen, which I think myself to be. Then the wounded man opened his eyes and called feebly to me, proving at least that I was not his assailant, 'I've been shot. I've been robbed. Help me.'

The policeman took my name and address and was obviously satisfied about my integrity. He and his companion carried the wounded man to the back of the patrol car and switching on the siren they drove away at emergency speed while the doctor I had summoned for help called complainingly from his apartment doorway, 'What's the hurry? Well I don't mind,' he said, when I explained. 'It's best for the police to remove these things from the street.'

Meanwhile the man's dog, which everyone had forgotten,

trailed helplessly entangled in its leash, barking and whining and showing only a brief interest in sexless Sally. I felt irritated that the dog should have been left behind. I felt as if I had done my duty in trying to help the wounded man. I was beginning to find in my street studies an untidiness, an incompleteness which angered me. I phoned to report a 'dog in distress'.

Then tugging at Sally's leash I led her back to the apartment, gave her a warm drink as if she were a child in shock after an unpleasant experience, saw her to her bed in the corner of the sitting room, then went to my own bed where Lenore lay half-asleep. I kissed her. I wanted her to forgive me. I wanted to make some promise to her which I knew I could never make.

'Tell me,' she said, half-asleep, 'how can I make those parents understand that some children are born unfinished, that the state of being unfinished is their natural state, that *we* have to do the finishing?'

Then she fell asleep. I slept too, and I dreamed of my grandfather and of Turnlung, and I dreamed of the man who had been wounded in the street. He was dying and attended, as we like to attend our dying, by many bottles and tubes with apparatus that resembled scaffolding, as if an extra body were being constructed beyond the real body, like those buildings where the shell is formed and visible while the interior is secretly demolished.

I woke with the image of the dog tangled in its leash running round and round whimpering for its master.

11

My next meeting with Turnlung was in the Natural History Museum which he said he would like to visit and although my favourite museum is the Metropolitan and I suggested meeting there, he insisted that he needed to see the animals 'in their setting'. He explained that in his country there was a dearth of indigenous animals and he felt his experience of life to be unfinished without his having seen and known some of the creatures of the past and present which he referred to as the 'easy mammals', comparing them with those of his own country which were often out of sight and inaccessible, making study of them difficult though possibly more rewarding.

'My country is Puritan, you know,' he said, laughing.

He said there were native spiders that one could learn to know and understand; also native bats and a number of birds, some wingless and nocturnal, and one prehistoric reptile; all these creatures, he said, held their drama within and would not easily surrender it, and though in old age one might accept challenges, he felt the need to have a less esoteric relationship with creatures.

'I mean,' he said, 'just to stand and look at a dead or living poisonous snake, or a simple carnivore.'

He arrived punctually at our meeting place near the bookshop. I was examining the postcards when I happened to look up and there was Turnlung making a small escaping leap from the revolving door, and so remarkable had he become in my life that I felt there to be something momentous even in that slight movement through the doors, as if they were not what they seemed and to enter and leave through them was to risk one's life.

He saw me almost at once. 'Ah,' he said.

His language was full of archaic exclamations, of Ohs and Ahs and My dears.

'Ah, my dear.'

It was almost unbelievable that I had met him only once before. We knew, and we knew that we knew our knowing of each other had been as long as a lifetime and our first meeting was merely a raising of the level of unconsciousness into consciousness or an ebbing of a tidal past to reveal the two aspects or ages of one landscape, two seasons under one sky. I kept seeing him at first as he appeared, then as he was transformed into myself, my father, my grandfather, becoming them and shedding their skins like a creature in metamorphosis, then becoming himself but retaining the other identities not because he chose to but because they attached themselves to him, like those plants which, lacking means to disseminate and reproduce alone, rely upon a stranger—man, beast, insect—to brush past them and unwittingly carry away their seed.

I studied his face again and again—the smooth soft skin, the neatly pointed grey beard, the thin strands of grey hair not quite concealing the blue-veined skull, vulnerable as a baby's, as if the fontanelle were not yet closed, and I thought of the newlyborn, how their organs, especially the vital organs—the heart, the lungs, the brain—are unfinished at birth, and yet having accepted life even they in their unfinished state must begin at once to struggle against death and secretly to complete their own birth—they, like the works of art, perfect through their built-in imperfections.

'Where shall we go?' Turnlung said. 'What shall we see?'

He spoke in a slightly patronising tone, as if I knew nothing. He referred to our meeting as 'an assignation'.

'What better place? ' he said, as I showed him the plan of the museum, 'than Reptile Hall?'

We walked up the stairs through the long corridor to the end wings. Turnlung consulted the blue-bordered map, tracing his finger along the blue lines.

'What would you like?' he said. 'Fish or snakes? Reptile Hall or Whale Valley?'

He was enthusiastic like a child.

'What marvellous museums you have! In the small town where I was brought up there was a whale skeleton suspended to the ceiling the whole length of the one room of the museum. I waited for it to fall but it never did; it was like an airship. It was the only life, to a dull small boy like me who hated museums; the whale, and in the centre of the room in a huge glass cube, a rebuilt bony-kneed moa with wicked expression in its glass eyes. To me, everything else was dead. I can't help admiring you Americans. You're great killers, death is your way of life, but you're also great reconstructors of what you've killed. Only God can do that and get away with it.'

We chose Reptile Hall. We decided we'd have time only for Reptile Hall, then we'd have something to eat in the restaurant.

'I get rather tired these days,' Turnlung said apologetically.

I read fear in his eyes.

'I live in the land that's like the Garden of Eden,' he said. 'But it can't be Eden without a snake. We're terrified it may become a true Eden. How we long to remain unharmed! And how carefully we identify the harm in the obvious places, without too much inner searching. We had a spider hunt recently when a black widow spider, a stowaway in the case of fruit, went on a spree to see the sights like any tourist. I think the troops might have been called out to get it.'

Turnlung thrust his face close to mine. His eyes were bright. I could not be sure if he was serious. 'Let me tell you,' he said.

'For a while it was touch and go. *Touch and go.* Somewhere among the ferns or the driftwood or on a city street corner there's a dead black widow. They called in experts to try decide whether it would be carrying eggs, and how spiders went about their sex life, in twos or ones or what have you.

'It was touch and go.'

Reptile Hall seemed to be darker than the other rooms. The display cases however were brightly lit, and coloured according to the habitat of the snakes which had been arranged in lifelike poses.

'The more lifelike it is,' Turnlung said, 'the more deathlike it becomes.'

He smiled. 'Excuse me if I bore you. As you know, death is my interest.'

'You know it's my interest, too,' I said, thinking that at last I would get some secret out of him, that he'd help me to get through a primer of death and beyond.

We walked, silent then, through Reptile Hall. Turnlung studied each showcase carefully, taking time to read the description of each species.

'I'd die,' he said, smiling at his out-of-context use, as it were, of the word 'die', 'if there were nothing to read in this Reptile Hall. That's another thing I like about this country of death. You're great confiders. When I'm sitting in the—you call it the *john?*—and read the information on the packet of bleach I feel like a priest who's heard a full confession. You give things so much life, you give them speech as well.'

'Tell me about yourself,' he said.

We were now in the restaurant eating egg salad sandwiches and drinking coffee and when Turnlung said, with some command in his tone, 'Tell me about yourself,' I felt like a small boy home for the vacation, being questioned by his grandfather.

Easily, prompted by his pertinent questions (he was insatiable for detail), I told him the story of my life. When his questioning became personal he made no apologies and I remember thinking I would get my revenge later by my own brand of questioning. I had read none of his writings. They were unobtainable, he said, in this country, and the way he said it gave the impression that we were living in a time of war, of great scarcity and peril. He was making a few notes, writing a few of his death experiences, he said. In words. He emphasised '*words*'. Not in music or paint. Words have much to account for, he said.

I suddenly thought with a feeling of loss, of my clean smooth father, the treasured paintings he bought each week, and his wistful hope that he'd 'like to meet the artist but why should an artist be interested in an ordinary businessman.' The paintings gave him so much pleasure. I could read the glee on his face as he unwrapped each package, like an obstetrician extracting an infant. I wondered, there in the restaurant, how much my father's acquiring of art was the search for the terms of death by a businessman used to business contracts who realised that the only contract that can be made with death is an imaginative one and therefore the place to search for the clauses of the contract is among the arts.

'I'm thinking of my father,' I said, in response to Turnlung's questioning glance. 'He looks for death among the images and the colours. You look among the words.'

I felt that I spoke possessively to Turnlung, as if I *knew* him. A flush of pleasure came into my face and I tried to hide it.

'The egg sandwiches,' I said. I blushed again.

When I had finished telling him about myself I did not feel as though I had emptied myself, only that I had been transferred to a kind of safe deposit, and when we parted we had arranged that I would visit him in his room on Thirty-fourth Street.

'Among the Funeral Homes,' he said slyly, referring, I supposed, to the fact that we had said very little about the topic which had been, we thought, the chief reason for our meeting again.

I went home to my apartment, patted Sally, made myself a bachelor tea. Lenore had left a note to say she would be out of town for several days. I was glad she had gone. I collected her few underthings and cosmetics and put them in a drawer of the dressing table, and I almost convinced myself that she no longer existed.

12

Today I walked with Talbot Edelman through Reptile Hall. I'm confused and tired. I feel like a young man in love for the first time. I find myself looking back into life when my intention is to look forward into death, yet even the words I use to write this are part of the great deceit and confusion: I imply that we move from There to Here, that we look backward to the past and forward to the future, but I could just as easily say, convincing myself, that we move round and round the source and the fountain. How we suffer from language! When I left Edelman outside the Natural History Museum it was not the colours and the patterns and the catalogued habits of the reptiles which haunted me in the midst of the central haunting by Edelman himself, it was the words, the names, recurring vividly to my mind.

Testitudines crocodylia, rhynchocephalia, squamata, sauria, serpentes, which repeated one after the other came to sound like an ancient prayer for the earliest forms of life.

Testitudines crocodylia, rhynochocephalia, squamata, sauria, serpentes...

Words, first words, are as traumatic as first love and first death. When we are young, presented with mature experienced words and lacking the mental imagery to receive them, we hospitably give them what we have in our minds only to find that we have invited them to live a falsehood which we believed to be truth. I am reminded of a word which caused much hope and suffering to me in my earliest years and which has accompanied me through my life, and because of its privileged metaphorical status, it will also attend my death. It is among the aristocracy of language because we have chosen to put it there.

The word is *jewel*.

I first heard the word 'jewel' when I was very young and its meaning was immediately clear, with the word becoming its meaning. Precious, a treasure, a glittering gem or stone in a choice of many colours and shapes and textures.

I knew that I would never own a jewel. I learned the names of jewels: ruby, sapphire, topaz, carnelian, fire opal, agate, moonstone, bloodstone, jasper, diamond. When my mother, in a poetic frame of mind, glanced out of the window in the early morning and observed that the lawn was covered with jewels I learned not to take her remark literally; nor when she spoke of a relative or friend as being a 'jewel', though I found it hard to accept these falsehoods and I resented the confusion I felt over my inability to discern where to put a word when it was given to me, whether among the real or the unreal, especially when to me all was real. I could say that by the time I was seven I had almost an open mind about language; I was prepared for any shock, and as vigilant as a soldier on sentry duty in my encounters with words, yet I was caught unawares at school one day, in my eighth year, when I overhead a fellow pupil say to his friend,

'In Class Two they sit in *jewel* desks. Class Two is the only classroom with *jewel* desks.'

You may imagine the effect of this news. From that moment I switched my hopes from dreams of Olympic glory (I was a fast runner) to those of acquiring a fortune in jewels. *Jewel desks.* In my saner moments I could not believe it was possible. My curiosity about the room with the jewel desks became intense and as I was too shy to ask for details I had to live in a torture of wondering, with at least the consolation that when I was promoted to Class Two my curiosity would be satisifed. When I passed the door to Class Two it was always closed, and I could hear murmurs from within, which I interpreted as murmurs of wonder and pleasure as Class Two inspected the jewels in a special hour devoted to jewel inspection and appreciation.

It began to seem impossible that I could live through the remaining three months of the year until I became eligible to share the jewels. I had a growing fear that the supply might end, as no doubt the jewels were distributed to Class Two pupils, on loan or permanently; I noticed some bulky school-bags being carried home in the afternoons. Also, I was worried about the evident secrecy. Except for that one day when I overhead the news I heard no one speak of the jewel desks. Once, casually, making it half a question, half a statement, I said to another boy, 'In Class Two you sit in a jewel desk.'

'Yeah,' he said. 'A jewel desk.'

He was uninterested, or he appeared to be; perhaps he had his own plans about the jewels and was confiding in no one.

One day when school was out and I was late going home I walked along the corridor and I was about to pass the room when I noticed the door was open and with an awful racing of my heart, I peeped in. I saw the desks, not single desks like ours, but long heavy desks with two lift-up seats to a desk. Not a jewel in sight. Obviously, they were removed each afternoon and locked in the class cupboard, and as if to confirm this, there was the teacher at that moment turning the key in the class cupboard. I had just missed seeing the jewels! It was almost as thrilling as having seen them.

Still, I might have gone crazy with wondering and planning had I not had an unexpected good fortune. One day, on the strength of being Excellent in Comprehension, Spelling and Arithmetic, and being able to recite unfalteringly in their correct order the ten longest rivers, highest mountain peaks, deepest lakes in the world, I, and Gloria Bone, were promoted to Class Two.

'You can move your books after school,' the teacher said. 'And go to Class Two tomorrow.'

After school we took our books to Class Two where, as I expected, the jewels were already locked away for the night.

'We'll be sitting in jewel desks,' Goria Bone said, so loudly that I hushed her.

'What do you mean, Sh-sh-sh? Everyone knows you sit in jewel desks in Class Two.'

I was alarmed. I saw my fortune disappearing. I dug Gloria Bone with my elbow which was effectively sharp. 'Blabber,' I said.

The teacher took our promotion cards to the class cupboard, opened it, put the cards quickly inside, and relocked it, seeming, to my inflamed imagination, to glance significantly at me as she turned the key in the lock. Her glance promised, Distribution for new pupils of sapphires, diamonds, rubies, carnelian, bloodstone, immediately after the Lord's Prayer and Hymn Singing tomorrow morning. What a stupendous promise! Nothing, I thought, must be allowed to interfere with the distribution of the jewels. Perhaps there would be a special hymn for the occasion,

> *When he cometh, when he cometh*
> *to make up his jewels,*
> *all his jewels, precious jewels,*
> *his loved and his own. . .*

Or perhaps we would sing that hymn where the reckless (how reckless!) saints were 'casting down their golden crowns around the glassy sea'.

There's a limit to patience. When I had been three days in Class Two and there was still no sign of the promised jewels I decided to ask about them. I said to my neighbour who sat with me in the new type of desk,

'I thought these were meant to be jewel desks.'

His reply mystified me. 'They *are* jewel desks. Can't you see?'

Here was a problem. It had not occurred to me that the jewels were invisible, the kind you read about, which could become visible if you were good, clever, self-sacrificing, courageous. Reluctant to admit that I might be none of these, I tried to new approach.

'Are you ever allowed to take them home? You know—a handful—to. . . to. . . (I was about to say to keep or to spend when I suspected this might be classified as unself-sacrificing) you know, to give to your mother so she can see again, or to your father so he can voyage round the world in his spare time.'

My classmate was matter-of-fact. He closed the lid of his desk carefully.

'I didn't know that your mother was blind or that your father was wanting to voyage around the world,' he said sarcastically.

'She isn't. He isn't.'

'Then what the heck are you talking about? I think you must be touched. What do you mean? A handful of what?'

Why could he not understand?

'Listen,' I said desperately. 'I'm talking about the *jewels* from the *jewel* desks, the *jewel* desks we're sitting in now.'

'Jewel desks? Jewel desks?'

Then he tittered down the scale, in sudden delight. 'You mean *duel* desks.' He spelled the world—d-u-e-l. 'Duel desks. Duel meaning two, a fight with swords. Fighting a duel. A duel desk. Are some people dumb! You don't mean you really thought these were jewel desks with diamonds and rubies and precious stones?'

His disbelief was infectious; I began to wonder if I had believed it myself. Diamonds, rubies, sapphires, agate, moonstone, bloodstones?

'Not exactly,' I said, a traitor to my dreams. 'Not exactly.'

It did not seem fair that one word could promise so much, could have held so much power to organise and disorganise my life. How could I have been so at the mercy of one word? My betrayal by the word 'jewel' was a lasting blow dealt to me by the language I was encouraged to be at home in.

That night when I came home from school I opened our dictionary and by chance found both the words *duel* and *dual*. I read, dual: pertaining to two, shared by two, twofold, double; duel: a combat between two persons fought with deadly weapons by agreement, in the presence of witnesses.

It's *dual* desks, I thought, realising that even my classmate, unknowingly, was a victim of the treachery of the language. His interpretation of 'duel' desks might cause him more suffering than mine had. Duel desks. Duel. A combat fought by two people with deadly weapons by agreement, in the presence of witnesses. He could be preparing a catastrophe for himself.

I prized the information given to me by the dictionary, and the generous way if offered up its words to anyone who turned its pages. I had never before prized information though I knew others did, and I was familiar with its power to grant victory in many battles both with other children and with adults. I realise now that I did receive the jewels I had been promised. I had opened the dictionary and I had been showered with the inescapable words which, if I worked, could become my allies instead of my enemies. The word 'jewel' remained with me in a special place among the indelible impressions of my life and it was like meeting a first love or a first hate when years afterwards, opening the English examination paper in the Public Service examination for accountants, I read, Paraphrase the following:

Dear beauteous death, the jewel of the just,
shining nowhere but in the dark.
What mysteries to lie beyond thy dust
could man outlook that mark!

There have been deaths in my life which touched the pressure points of my experience, enriching it as if by fine jewels (the word serving me at last) which in their new setting revealed more clearly their own brilliance, density, perfections and imperfections. The idea of death as a jewel seems to me fair recompense for my painful association with the word; it allows me to indulge in an exquisite annihilation of the togetherness in which it once disguised itself. Dual indeed! Or duel! A combat fought by agreement with deadly weapons, in the presence of witnesses.

It is good to see death returning to Class Two where, imagining we sit together, we sit alone.

13

All day, after my meeting with Talbot Edelman, I have been in a feverish state. On my way home I called at the library and searching for the numbers on the shelves I read GOD which on closer inspection I found to be 800—Literature. I left the library and caught the downtown bus and beside me sat a young man studying a folio. He took a pen from his pocket and began to write as if he were seated at a desk instead of in a swaying jolting bus. Seeing someone in the act of writing has always given me joy. Those who write are alone, they are not in a team, like footballers and cricketers and tennis players, or in twos like animals escaping to the Ark, or in multiples like members of Parliament or in twelves like members of a jury. We need our solitary workers—our writers, painters, composers. We need also the gardeners, fishermen, lighthouse keepers, tightrope walkers.

The faces of the people on the bus were sour and pale and someone near me kept farting, and the smell filled the bus. I glanced down at the young man's writing. I read AGONY. In capital letters. Here was a writer, I thought, surviving the city gas smells and the public transport farts; writing the relevant word: AGONY.

I'm a stupid old man at times. As in the nonsense poem, I have spent a large part of my life being the man who thought he saw, and who looked again. It has been my work.

He thought he saw an elephant addressing him in Greek.
He looked again and saw it was the middle of next week.

I looked again at the young man's writing. I saw that he had made a column of figures and it pleased me to think (after my years in accountancy) that these should be headed by the word AGONY. I glanced again at the heading. Of course. It was not AGONY. It was the numeral 1800. Not 1800 agonies.

Eighteen hundred dollars. The young man was calculating his profit and loss.

Yet I felt as those who are mad or in love feel, that GOD in the public library and AGONY in the public transport among the farts and the sour-faced farters and the haemorrhoid advertisements had some special message for me.

How tired I have been! I came home then to my room here in Thirty-fourth Street. It is a decayed street, littered with papers and broken bottles. The iron railings leading up the steps to the houses are twisted as only the monsters in the films know how to and are expected to twist and deform wrought iron. Although my landlady, a Scotswoman who has her quarters in the basement, keeps a clean house she has not been able to get rid of the rooming-house smell, a mixture of leaking gas, burnt milk, bathroom odours and, each day, the peculiar residual smell of the day before which by evening is masked by the maturing smells of that day and arranged, like cheeses, on the landings, the hallways, and outside the door to each room.

My room is on the third floor facing the back garden with two windows one of which opens. The trees now are showing mists of green although their bark still holds the blackness that is the legacy from the other side of the snow, long past. My room has a convertible bed, a number of folding metal trays painted with red flowers, a small table, bookshelves, vases of everlasting flowers, the kind which crumble at a touch, scattering their lifeless ornamental seeds; and plastic flowers which shine and sweat in the warmth of the radiator, switched on to lessen the cold of the evenings. One corner of my room has a cooking ring attached by an extension cord to an outlet so far away that when I switch on the power I can almost see it wake, yawn, then set out on its long slow journey along the cord. Beneath the cooker there are cupboards for dishes and pans and beside it, a sink with a cold water tap or faucet as it is known here. My bathroom is off the landing and it too has the characteristic smell which breeds here.

The room is quiet except for the hissing of the radiator and the sound of the traffic, and I've set up my typewriter by the closed window and I try to write these death notes regularly, though since my meeting with Talbot Edelman, first near Lincoln Centre, and now, today, at the Natural History Museum, my writing has lapsed. I grow so tired lately. There have been sudden frightening blanks in my memory. I become confused, not knowing which city or country I am living in, and I break out in a sweat as I try to think clearly, and my hands begin to shake as the fear grows, and I ask myself, Is this the state for an old man like myself to be involved with anything but a clear search for death? In the past I have believed in discovery through looking away, that the direct pursuit and capture of a dream or an idea may lead to the disintegration of the dream. I had thought that if I had been living at the time of Icarus I might have witnessed his fall from the sky because I might have been gazing away from the centre of my preoccupation. I feel now, however, that I have so little time to haunt the circumference, the horizon, when I am here at the end, at the centre, the foreground. I must look directly at my death.

Even my progress around the city on foot is slower than I planned. Most excursions are beyond me unless I take the bus. When I set out toward the rivers, taking the crosstown bus part of the way, I found that there was no place to *be*, and this, within my waking dream of death, seemed ominous. The two rivers flow farther and farther from the streams of man and if a man can get to stand near them he realises that the water does not even grant him a shadow, nor does it grant a shadow to the city, while the sun itself cannot dredge from it a light-glimmer of gold. The city rivers, filled with death, have long ago given up speaking of death; indeed, they are so far past speaking of it that as a kind of seasonal irony, in springtime, they allow a green and yellow fire of grass and forsythia to break out along the riverbanks of the Hudson Valley, above the opaque polluted waters, flaunting the green and yellow life that bears the seeds of decay.

For the first time I am beginning to question my visit here. I try to understand why a country, an abundant mother, which has fed so many of the hungry and the poor should at the same time continue to secrete the milk of death. I try to understand death itself, with inadequate language that is forced to make an excursion into metaphor and returns changed, emaciated, impoverished or enriched, often too powerful for its alphabet. I keep seeing Talbot Edelman's pale handsome face, his dark eyes full of sadness and hope, his gaunt body set almost in a pose of a letter of the alphabet, the abject M, the military R, the lonely nude I; as if he were an adjunct and instrument of language. How strange that one who has had so little personal acquaintance with death should have the qualifications to issue a certificate of death. Is he a dream? Will he grow old and wise and much loved?

O Natrix septemvittata Lampropeltis Crotalus ruber Crotalus viridus cerberus elaphe obsoleta thamnophis elegans natrix cyclopion, coluber constrictor, and the heterodon platyrhynos who plays dead.

14

I visited Turnlung in his room. I took unusual care in dressing for my visit. I wore my corduroy waistcoat, the kind that was in fashion then, and I used a Russian brand of cologne, and my mirror told that in my smart clothes and with my dark eyes and hair and sallow skin I looked handsome and Russian, and certainly not as if I were a member of the Department of Death studies about to pursue my research.

Turnlung's street was a dreary place littered with pieces of stone from unseen wrecked buildings, and the glass of broken bottles, and squelched beer cans. I could see the Funeral Homes with their crematoria chimneys adding a share of sky that one might have spoken of innocently, in past times, as clouds. I could see the corner delicatessen with the street outside stained with blood and sauerkraut; and the sad-eyed junkies sitting in the doorways. Turnlung's area of street was cleaner, housing a small group of landladies who were evidently obsessive polishers, wipers and sweepers. I arrived at the 'cocktail hour'.

'I've this wine,' Turnlung said. 'Made from grapes and guavas. It's call *Grava*.'

He poured a glass each. He appeared to be nervous and he

moved with small hopping steps and I felt myself staring at him with a sudden cold anger, I did not know why.

'You have no live plants,' I said, thinking after I had spoken that I sounded accusing.

He pointed to the vases of artificial everlasting flowers. 'My landlady furnished these. The back apartments have these, the front apartments have living plants, don't ask me why. To give an impression, I suppose. These are everlasting flowers.'

He reached out and touched one. It crackled. 'They last for ever but they break easily. See, there are crumbs of them everywhere.'

The carpet beneath them was scattered with brown crumbs like toast crumbs.

'This is good wine,' I said, feeling self-conscious, like a student drinking for the first time with a member of the faculty. We sat, each in an armchair, sipping our wine and staring at each other. Turnlung looked tired. My inexplicable anger changed to pity as I thought of his age. I tried to suppress the pity because I had been careful to explain in the geriatric department that old age was no more to be pitied than was childhood or middle age, no more than the seasons were to be thought of as separate disasters or revelations, that each held their sadness and joy, but you may be sure that these comparisons with the seasons were not accepted by my city students, while I myself was suspicious of them.

They were vivid in my mind because when I became aware that I once had an 'official' boyhood, the associations of my time at home became inseparable from memories of snow and sun, leafed and bare boughs, a lake of ice and snow that I could skate upon without danger, and the same lake, transformed, where I canoed and fished. Each seasonal memory held sharp pain and pleasure not always in direct proportion to the age of the year, for the midsummer outward heaven brought the inner hell of summer camp, and the dead grip, the rigor mortis of winter released a flying life in me as I skated whirling and leaping across the lake, the blood surging to the tips of my fingers and toes and ears and my face rosy with the blood-blush of pure being. I remember once, as if on an impulse to match the summer heaven with an offering from the summer hell where I had been confined, on my last day at summer camp, as I set out alone on the train journey toward the city, I flung my suitcase, opened, from the door of the train and I watched the rushing wind of air and railroad catch up my clothes in its arms in a joyous acceptance, before distributing sweaters, socks, underwear, upon the dogwood bushes and the glossy carpet of poison ivy.

Looking at Turnlung, seeing the slight tremor in his hands as he held the wineglass and the marked beat of the pulse in his temple, I found my preaching was no use to me: I did pity him. I pitied his old age. He brushed the wine from his lips, and it seemed as if the wine itself knew that at Turnlung's age the body which is mostly water finds it hard to control its natural impulse to flow, to obey the command of the current of age when the dams which hold the body fluids are likely to burst or leak or overflow; and thus even the wine and coffee and tea are spilled and slopped. 'His time is running out,' we say of an old man, thus giving a realistic description of the last years of his life, the sense of the body's flowing outward, of the one, no longer self-contained, becoming the many.

'I'm quite busy with writing my death experiences,' Turnlung said. 'My first book was called First Death. This is to be Last Death. My own. I believe in making the journey, the search, the discovery. I want my last years to have the real dream, the real journey. It is a preparation for leaving, for vacating myself.'

Then he smiled and tapped his head. 'I shall hope to keep my furniture as long as possible, and to use it. The drapes are not necessary; they serve only to obscure the growth of the light and the dark; they shelter, yet deceive; with the drapes gone, I discover corners of the room I never knew existed.'

Listening to him, even pitying him in his age, I was overcome by my own weakness and youth. He was my grandfather. I had a sense of our walking side by side through a vast almost empty house inspecting each room, the boy listening, his heart beating with terror and apprehension, while the grandfather made a mournful tally of the furniture that remained and from time to time spoke angrily, almost incoherently, about the removers who were at work, shadowy presences going stealthily from room to room as if to mock Grandfather's careful inventory. The rooms were drenched with light as it rained through the bare windows, lapped against the walls, and flowed to every dark corner. Soon it would be dark with complete true darkness, as all the light fittings had now been removed from the house; the bulbs had been taken violently from their sockets, the source of heat had been cut off, there was no way to make or store food, no comfortable place anymore to lie or sit; it was impossible to sleep, and a torture to be awake; it was time to leave, if the boy and his grandfather knew of a place to go. Did they know of such a place?

I felt myself full of pity and love. Tears flowed down my cheeks. A look of panic came into Turnlung's face. He eyes were glistening with tears. Then we lay down, embracing, on the sofa. We lay there the remainder of the afternoon. I had never felt such grief or sadness or comfort. The room grew dark. The lights began to show in the apartment buildings facing the room; figures moved against the frames of light like figures in a painting who come alive, briefly, change their posture, then settle again for another eternity.

When I returned to my apartment I felt light-headed and very lonely. I had a cup of tea and some cookies. I looked about the ugly apartment. I felt gratitude for the furniture, the rugs and the bedding, the light fixtures, the utensils in the kitchen, waiting to be used; and the stove's alabaster gleam.

I switched on all the lights and I slept with all the lights burning, like a child who is afraid of the dark.

The next day I wandered aimlessly with Sally in Central Park. I was filled with a sense of loss. I felt as if I had begun a period of mourning, as if I were waiting for the first letters of sympathy to arrive, for I needed to answer them. Lenore had suddenly become transformed in my mind to a kind of witch brewing an evil brew from the unfinishings of her small patients. My thoughts were bizarre. The images ran like watercolours in my mind; everything, including myself, seemed to lose substance, beginning to flow, slowly at first then swiftly as if reaching a place of hidden rapids. Finally I went home and slept again. I hoped that Turnlung would phone me, for I had given him my number. He did not phone.

The next day my thoughts were clearer. I though of Lenore with loss and regret, as if she had died. I had an impulse to write her a long melancholy letter about woods in the fall and the old age of the imagination. I felt myself to be waiting for a diversity of departures and arrivals, for freight within myself to be sent on to its destination and for me to collect that which was addressed to me, officially receiving and unpacking it. I had never before been so conscious of the unfinished nature of my world and my life; I longed to accept every finishing touch, even that of my own death.

Turnlung phoned that afternoon. The voice sounded far

away, then it died. I spoke to the operator.

'There's someone trying to talk to me. He can't get through.'
The operator's voice was cool. 'Is it a distant party?'

'No,' I said sharply. 'It's not a long-distance party. It's here,
in this city.'

'Do you know the number?' she asked.

'No.'

'I'm sorry I can't help you. Are you sure it's not a distant
party?'

I put down the receiver. A few minutes later the phone rang
again. It was Turnlung.

'I was cut off,' he said. He sounded full of life and health and
his voice transmitted sudden joy to me, dispelling all my fears
and anxieties.

'How have you been?' I asked him.

'Fine, fine. Talbot?'

'Yes?'

'Say my name.'

'Your name?'

'My name. Turnlung.'

I obeyed him. 'Turnlung.'

'Say it slowly.'

'Turnlung.'

'You know what it means?'

I hesitated. He had not told me but I knew. 'A state of
readiness for death, I suppose,' I said.

'I've felt a great peace,' he said.

There was a pause. He said, 'Are you afraid?'

'No,' I said. 'I've been confused but I don't think I'm afraid.'

'Shall we meet then, tomorrow, at Central Park Zoo, to look
at the live animals?'

We arranged to meet at the zoo, under the clock. We said

a luxuriously formal goodbye over the phone, as if we were indeed long-distance parties.

15

It was an unseasonable day with each season contributing a sample of weather. Turnlung and I arrived at Central Park Zoo in fall, lunched in spring and winter, and parted in summer, in a tantalising succession of inappropriate outward suns and storms, for I was aware that our inward seasons kept strictly to the classical order, where trees bud before they come to leaf, and leaves fall before the woods decay and the chilly days of lemon-coated sun both preceded and follow the scorching days of foundry-furnace sun.

Turnlung looked frail in a backwoodsman shirt he said he had picked up at a dime store. When he spoke to me he said, 'My dear,' like an old-fashioned father addressing his daughter, or—the comparison came to mind—a tired old man talking to his aged wife. We had lunch. We were both hungry and we ate in silence, glancing at each other now and again as photographers glance at their subjects, to get the general effect and pose and atmosphere and judge the light. Then we glanced down at our food, adjusting it on the plate as if it were indeed a kind of camera. The air was clear, full of clatter, the working of giant engines, the screaming of sirens and from nearby the occasional bellows and roarings and trumpetings of the animals. Turnlung seemed to be listening to no sound but the animal sounds. A look of excitement came over his face when the lion roared. He could barely wait to finish his lunch.

'Let's go to the animals,' he said.

Briefly he escaped from my focus and I saw just a lonely old man with nothing better to do than go to stare at the animals. I felt ashamed of my momentary view of him. Who was I, then? I asked myself, but a lonely younger man going to stare at the animals, perhaps to surprise them in the midst of sex because I hadn't found many satisfactions of my own.

And what was all this lofty talk of death? I asked myself, when, if the truth were known ...

'It's never known,' Turnlung said, answering a remark I had not even voiced.

We walked through the cat house, stopping at each cage to admire the grace and courage evident in spite of the habitual attitude of imprisonment that replaced brightness in the eyes with bewilderment and a perpetual leaking from the tear ducts that looked very much like real tears for real reasons, and the sleek coat with dull dry tufts of fur. We stopped by the old toast-brown lion, commiserating with it. Its head appeared abnormally large in the small cage with the mane resembling a growth prompted by endocrine imbalance rather than by essential lionhood. The flesh on its hind legs hung loose like the shanks of an old man, and the testicles were dropped and withered, almost brushing the floor of the cage.

'He's a real old codger,' Turnlung said admiringly.

'He needs a bath,' I said, surprised at my sudden prim interest in cleanliness which I felt I'd had too much of in my life. 'He stinks.'

'Too right he does. They all stink. It's the real prison stink. I wonder what feelings about us they release with this stink. No offence to your city, my dear, but it reminds me of all those hostile New Yorkers farting away on their public transport.'

We came then to the buffalo enclosure containing, so the notice said, a female and her daughter of six months standing in the shelter of her mother on the moulting patch of grass, with an expression of bewilderment exactly like her mother's: a family conspiracy of sullen bewilderment.

'They look pretty lonely standing there,' Turnlung said. 'As if they'd been offered the world, the earth and the sky, and they had to refuse, and couldn't explain the refusal. The baby's aged a lot in six months.' He spoke tenderly, as if it were a human child.

We turned away from the buffaloes because, suddenly, neither of us could face their quiet immobility and patience and the bewilderment wearing away their lives as the pressure of their bodies was wearing away the grass of their enclosure, until unless artificial turf were laid, the grass would be unlikely to grow again. We joined the crowd to watch the seals swimming and leaping and barking in a way that could be interpreted, gratefully, as approval of the human race, if one were in a self-congratulatory mood. We relaxed. The crowd clapped and laughed its enjoyment. In my mind, for I can never quite forget my profession, I compared the seals to some people I had known—plump with small eyes and tight-fitting skin.

We walked under the archway where a shelved telephone had been torn from its socket and the chained telephone book ripped apart and the pages scattered in the corner in a pool of urine. Everywhere in the city, Turnlung remarked, there were these traces of hostility, attacks on the inanimate world by the body acting as agent for the soul, because, he said, unlike in olden times when a man's soul could fly freely out of his body into the spaces of air and sky and return at will, now his sould was confined within, and it if risked flight it was liable to be destroyed as those birds are which fly unknowingly, blindly, into skyscrapers and passing planes because they are unable to grasp the fact of their substance.

'So much for the soul,' Turnlung said, as we went into the men's room and stood side by side, glancing down at each other like two schoolboys making the important comparison, I hurriedly finished and zipped my fly. Turnlung dribbled on for a few minutes then he zipped up. I had an image of him naked, and then of him enclosed in the underwear that old men use in winter, like a second skin, that you could lift up and pinch between your finger and thumb as the flesh and fat had gone from them, and then I remembered there had been just such an old man recently in one of the geriatric wards; wearing buttoned underwear, yellowish-white, the same colour as milk from a newly calved cow or the first drops from a woman's breast. The old man had died, and his body has been so shrunken that I had to search for it beneath the underwear, and I remembered that I kept discovering bones and muscles here and there as if each were an isolated part and all had been brought together as a final collection for the exhibition or ceremony of death.

We walked from the alcove along the path leading to the entrance to the park where the buggies were drawn up, the black blinkered horses stamping in their eagerness to get away, their working coats glossy in the sun, for summer had come and the cold wind that had trailed and encircled us during lunch had died leaving the air still, with the sun shining directly above us, like a reading lamp thrust close.

'I feel,' Turnlung said happily, 'as if this were the Indian summer of my life. Selwyn, my old friend, died some years ago, and I've been alone since then. We were dear to each other. We were the same age, we had the same memories, we could quote the same news from the same old newspapers. Age touched him faster than it touched me. If catastrophe or sickness or happiness came to us it was always his body that recorded it, writing details here and there, capriciously. Since I've been in New York I myself have aged a great deal. But you, my boy, are young.'

I listened as he repeated the cliche I'd been hearing most of my life until I wondered at what age would it become meaningless: 'At your age you have all your life before you.'

He smiled as he said it, as my grandfather would have smiled, I thought, then I tried to dismiss the thought of Grandfather, I tried to give Turnlung a place of his own, not to fit him into the pattern of others; and yet I had not forced him; he simply fitted; like the old men in winter who used to make angels by lying in the snow with arms outstretched and, standing, yet leaving the pattern of themselves, with wings, so my father and my grandfather were lying down in Turnlung's life, leaving their pattern imprinted on him, and such was the mysterious, increasing power my grandfather held over me, that he could have had wings, and angelic properties.

'When Selwyn died,' Turnlung said, 'and he was lying in his coffin, I felt that if I suddenly looked away, and he climbed out, it would have been the most natural gesture for me to climb in, even to allow the coffin to be closed and myself to be buried in Selwyn's place. But whatever are we talking about, young man? Who are you? I'm very agile for my age.'

At first I thought his sudden change of mood was a joke. Then I saw that he looked ill, and confused.

'I think I'd better sit down,' he said. 'I feel strange.'

I took his arm and steered him toward the wooden benches near the entrance to the park, and sat him down.

'Yes, I'm very agile for my age,' he said. 'And I'm not one of those who can't remember when they last had an erection, though mind you it's not what it used to be. I think I'm feeling old,' he said. He looked afraid.

The condition, which Turnlung referred to as a 'spell', giving it a magical origin, passed quickly and we both sat silent and chastened and perhaps resentful of the hint of the death which we were pleased to think of in the abstract, as the rich think of 'the poor' or the developed countries plan for and solve the problems of the 'underdeveloped' countries. I had thought that Turnlung with his literary interest in death and I with my scientific research were different, as the 'experts' are supposedly different: I saw that we were not. I felt tired, much older than my years, as if Turnlung in his moment of desperation had given some of his years into my keeping—hold these years while I get my wits about me!—and had forgotten to reclaim them. I began to worry about him. What if he should fall ill, alone in this country, with no relatives, no friends except me? Where could he go? There must be some place for him, I thought.

There must be some place for him.

My mother's words. Speaking of Grandfather. I at least was not like the rest of my family; I was different.

'My apartment,' I said recklessly. 'You could stay in my apartment. There are two small rooms off the big studio room. The back garden is pretty, with trees. There's an engine of some kind working ceaselessly; it may trouble you; I can't discover what it is or where exactly the sound comes from. I feel that each apartment in that building has been assigned a number of irritations of sight and sound and smell, as a part of the lease. I need not stay there. I've been thinking of moving.'

There must be some other place for him. My mother again. Speaking of Grandfather.

Turnlung looked nervous as if he had heard my mother's voice in my mind.

'What about your woman—Lenore? Will she understand?'

'Sure she'll understand. She'll understand but I don't know what she'll feel. We've lost what we had, if we ever had it,' I said, concentrating my gaze on two squirrels who were fighting over a piece of bread as if it were their last picking to see them through a long winter. They clawed at each other.

'Their claws are sharp,' I said. 'Oh yes, Lenore and I have worked well together at the clinic. I suppose the only women I really feel anything for,' I said carefully, 'are those who are either unobtainable or not interested.'

'What about men?'

'They're safe,' I said.

'You mean you're safe with them.'

'I guess so.'

I made an effort to get back on the tracks of illness and death. 'Are you still feeling ill?'

'Fine, I'm fine.'

I could hear the helplessness and panic in his voice.

We sat in the summer of the park. The sun was steadily coaxing the leaves to unfurl from their timid spring postures, their foetal secrecy; the squirrels scurried about in their original grey fur coats, their rat-faces cunningly watching the people on the benches, calculating the prospect of food, their lustrous tails which elevated them from the rat family and gave them the approved status of squirrels, billowing and brushing behind them. Everything, everyone blossomed in the sun which also cast a spell over the memory of the city violence, banishing it. The junkies, derelicts, pushers, hustlers occupying the benches cooperated by assuming an inanimate stillness like pieces of scenery, remnants of another act in another drama which had been left for dismantling and removal. One old man, unshaven, with large-pupiled dark eyes lay the length of the seat next to us, looking up at the mild sky. His mouth was open and every time he breathed he appeared to exhale blue smoke which, with his ragged dishevelment, caused him to look like a fall bonfire reassembled in the shape of a human being. I looked at him. I felt the taut compassion that the old and sick and helpless have always roused in me. Then I looked at Turnlung, coming home to him as to a familiar place. I did not object to his giving me some of his years to carry.

He drew attention again to his backwoodsman shirt.

'Do you like it?'

He began plucking at the sleeve and a feeling of dread came over me as, trained to read the sign language of sickness, I recognised the familiar plucking gesture of one in delirium. Turnlung, however, was not delirious.

'Back home,' he said. 'This is the idea of the American dress. Checked shirt on the body, a hamburger or gum in the mouth, dollars in the pocket, central-heating softness on the skin, and greed, greed, greed in the eyes. Oh, and oil, oil in the blood. Not pretty. Does it suit me, this shirt?' He posed for me to get the general effect.

'You have a face like a medieval scholar,' I said. 'And you're dressed like a lumberjack, a butcher...'

'Am I? I think I could find some argument to equate those with a writer. I've become practised in wedging a writer wherever I can into society, just to give him a place of his own though he may even then be in the shadow of another profession. Whereas you—I don't think your profession is so versatile. Do you find it satisfying? You've a sensitivity I should have thought would be rare. You have to be tough.'

'I *am* tough. Look at the way I've performed surgery on my dog Sally.'

'Well, you're fond of her,' he said, to my surprise, 'therefore you find it easier to hurt her.'

'That's not the point,' I said hurriedly. 'She's always been anaesthetised. There's no question of hurting.'

'There's lasting mutilation, though. Don't you care?'

'Yes. I care. We've grown very close.'

He looked slyly at me. 'What of the rest of your work—the deaths—which, by the way, are the meeting or hunting ground of our friendship?'

'You become immune to the deaths.'

'Oh? Do you know, my dear, that if you put the words "immune" and "inhuman" together you may make *immune*, *inhuman*, and *H-men*. Who are the H-men?'

'Anyone, especially a writer, can play tricks with words,' I said impatiently. 'It's his profession.'

'And you don't play tricks with genes, chromosomes, medicines, bloodtypes, adding a little something here, subtracting a little, finding the difference, magnifying it, diminishing it? You don't play tricks with mice, giving them a universe, believing them to be men while you play God?'

'With genes and so on,' I said, 'there's a risk and a responsibility if you start tampering with them.'

'Words are a risk, too. The first risk. And they've been tampered with before they get into the language, before birth; their very birth is a tampering.'

'We give the risk to the rats and mice,' I said.

'And the loved ones, like Sally the dog.'

'Yes. But what about the big tricks played by words?'

'The word "death," ' Turnlung said, 'is one of the bigger

tricks. How does one know where or how to search for the truth, which is also a trick-word? It's futile going to the planets and the moon, though it's a diverting wonder, and when the poets get there it will be a verbal indulgence that will only give the tyrant language more power to deceive. Should we not be travelling to investigate the tongue and its tides and phases?

'As for death,' he said, musing, and began to quote:

> Dear beauteous death, the jewel of the just,
> shining nowhere but in the dark.
> What mysteries do lie beyond thy dust
> could man outlook that mark!

'Jewel is a treacherous word.'

He spoke with an intensity that made me wonder if he'd had an unpleasant experience with jewels or jewel investment. Perhaps in his days of accountancy he had been reckless? I doubted it. Turnlung impressed me as a natural man in the sense that he lived with enough food, enough clothing, enough shelter and no more; as trees live, without suddenly doubling their quota of leaves for fear they have none the following year, or contriving to attract a triple share of sunlight, though trees do steal light and food from neighbouring trees.

'Yes, jewel is a treacherous word,' Turnlung repeated.

'So we've agreed,' he said triumphantly, 'that you and I are both deceivers working with deceivers, in the dark.'

'It depends on how paranoid you are,' I said.

Turnlung looked afraid. 'I should go home now,' he said. 'Back to my room. *Agile* can so easily become *fragile*. Just think of those two letters *f* and *r* loitering in the doorway.

'We'll kiss now,' he said, and surprised me by kissing me on the lips. 'Will you get me a cab, my dear?'

He sounded impossibly Victorian. His lips had felt like softened sealing wax. Neither my father nor my grandfather had kissed me in that way, and I thought of them at that moment as men without lips, with gums only, and teeth, and no power, lipless, to kiss or to speak the words I wanted to hear, not even to speak *me*, as if I had been a word, a sound enclosed in the skin-letter of an alphabet. I was I, the pillar and post and stake—how mysterious it was, this effect on me of Turnlung's presence and absence.

'Phone me,' I said, as the cab began to move away. 'And don't forget about my apartment.'

When he had gone I felt very lonely. I retraced my steps back to the cages of the cats. I stood by the buffalo enclosure. I felt deserted and confused and remote from my death studies. I spent the rest of the afternoon wandering around the city and when I returned to my apartment Lenore had arrived back and was fast asleep on the sofa in the studio and I wondered what sudden delicacy or modesty had prevented her from sleeping in my bed. I found a message by the telephone.

'A Mr Turnlung phoned and sent his love.'

I went to my room, without waking Lenore, though Sally, not having had her walk, whimpered restlessly but did not get up from her bed.

I slept with the bedroom door closed.

16

Should I, who am not Lear, apportioning my estate
be proud that I have signed it over to senility?
I had only one daughter, a furry buffalo
of six months, already trained to bewilderment,
immobility upon a counterfeit earth. The trees
are filled with yellow lions falling bodiless through the light
their parchment skin peeled away, summer-burned.
But the topic on which I am meaning to write
is death. I did not know it was searching for me
while I re-searched. The immortal flowers sweat. The heat
is central in the matured buildings of innersprung mattresses
and windows that refuse to open to let out the lassitude of
    sleep.
Heat, parks, railway stations are Central and Grand.
Talbot Edelman has a white smooth-pebbled hand.
The child, the lion and the buffalo are all burned.

I pray for my memory. Who am I,
Am I an H-man inhumanly immune

whose fragile agility rose like an army to quell
love lying weaponless at the bottom of the well?

Who am I? In which room shall I sleep tonight?
Shall I, waking, identify myself in the daylight?
A self of which city? Which country? I am being fleeced
    like a sheep
of my wits, the only warmth I have really wanted to keep.

* * *

Mice are not men, everyone is happily saying.
Then why are the mice praying?

Men are not Gods everyone was saying
when the mice began praying to the men.
Out of this mixture why say No No
to my daughter, the bewildered buffalo?

Walking in Central Park I suffered a spell.
Turnlung, Talbot said, you're not looking very well.

I'm witnessing a death, to myself I said.
I'm one of the twelve citizens, specially invited.

We sat in the park, directly under the sun.
I hired a dream. I kissed my companion.

Rapid the cab that drove me from the beasts and men.
My Daughter Buffalo called, Dad are you ever coming to
    me again?

I was firm. Never, never, from my cab I cried.
But I lied.

How can I possibly leave the world so good
unless imagining a great flood
I flee with Talbot and my Daughter Buffalo to an ark
of death rising out of the rock in Central Park?

17

When I woke the next morning I heard Lenore preparing breakfast in the kitchen and I was surprised that, knowing I was home, she had not crept into bed with me. I have always disliked the morning, it is too responsible a time, with the daylight demanding that it be 'faced' and (usually when I wake for I wake late) with the sun already up and in charge of the world, with little hope of anyone usurping or challenging its authority. A shot of light in the face of a poor waking human being and another slave limps wounded into the light-occupied territory.

I'd say that I then had two slaves myself—Sally was scratching and whimpering at my closed door while Lenore was setting the breakfast things on the table. Lenore's efficiency and neatness reminded me of my mother's habits, though she lacked my mother's intensity and maturity of feeling, the kind that develops perhaps through the fulfilment of maternal desires, and is assisted by the experience of the physical abandonment of sex and giving birth which, with the behavioural intruder, homicide, are signposts to the final abandonment of dying. Time and again in the O. and G clinic, a woman, stirruped and exposed for examination while I lean over her with my exploratory interrogatory searchlight, has confessed, This is the end; and when the child is born, doctor, goodbye dignity for ever.

The loss of dignity is equated with humiliation, also with a certain freedom of becoming, a substitution of mores imposed by society for a newly discovered, comprehended and accepted, life code. I always felt, sadly, that my own mother had squandered her richness of being on her care for the house and its furniture and utensils and machines, with the human inhabitants, somewhat like in a comic movie where mannequins are mistaken for people, talked to and dusted, spring-cleaned and cared for, in a similar way.

Lying in bed thinking of Lenore and of my mother and analysing them in cold waking fashion I regretted that I would not be able to observe the blossoming of Lenore. I would have enjoyed seeing the components of her personality acted upon by sex and childbirth, their changing, strengthening, weakening, with I, as the chemist in the laboratory, taking an occasional sip of the woman-brew, not as part of its mixture, but as the chemist only; or, if involvement were found to be necessary, as the spoon dipped in to stir the solution, then taken out and washed till no trace of the solution remained. It then occurred to me that a rat or white mouse could be substituted for Lenore, without much loss to her or to myself.

The shocking fact of this thought woke me completely. I had the same fear when I held the abortion brains in their plastic bag and realised that they felt little different from an ordinary package I had bought at the supermarket, going through the usual emotionless procedure of wheeling the shopping cart in and out of the cart traffic, pausing at the indicated shelves, noting the price, choosing, taking my time to decide which check-out counter was most suitable—the normal or the Express, Eight Items or Less; and then emerging with the feeling that invariably overcomes me there, of dehumanisation; for I remember what my race experienced, and sometimes as a child in our clean home I would dream of what I had heard of the concentration camps, the time and motion studies put into effect to enable an inmate to go from one place fully clothed, and, divesting himself of everything without and much within, arrive at the end-place with nothing, yet with an economic completeness for death; and I felt the strange parallel of the supermarkets where instead of divesting ourselves of goods we collect them, we arrive laden at the exits where, exchanging our money for goods and receiving the green or blue stamp blessing, we come out into the street with the hope that in some way we have replaced the processions of death with those of life.

Just then Lenore and Sally came into my bedroom though the commotion was mostly Sally's and as soon as I saw her I knew that she was sick.

'Keep back, Sally,' Lenore said.

Sally drew back obediently and lay with her head between her paws facing me. She was shivering and her rump had a peculiar cramped pose. Then without warning she went into a convulsion. Her mouth foamed and at last she lay rigid.

I did not stop to respond to Lenore's cherry-tasting morning kiss. I leaped out of bed and I crouched beside Sally and felt for a pulse, and my penis cocked its head, as if listening.

'Sally's dying,' I said.

I knew it was a miracle she had lived so long, especially after the strain of the cardiology experiments. It was a great pity, I had thought, when in my work I should have rejoiced, that a dog's heart is so close to the human heart in its functioning.

I dressed quickly and I was glad I'd slept late as the vet would be in his office. My medical treatment of Sally had always been carried out on the assumption that she was a human being and my knowledge of veterinary science was limited. Sally, once she had the usual doggy shots and dewormings, had become, in my eyes, a human being. I phoned the vet, describing the symptoms. Sally, still on the bedroom floor, was unconscious.

The vet was abrupt. 'I don't feel, from what you say, that there's anything I can do. You seem to have settled her yourself with those mutilations. The kindest thing is to send her to the Dogs' Heaven.'

In my feverish state I really believed for a moment that there was such a place as a dogs' heaven.

'The Dogs' Heaven?'

'The Dogs' Heaven. It's a small tasteful funeral parlour in the neighbourhood of Thirty-fourth Street, among the ordinary funeral homes. The clients prefer it that way. It's very discreet. The dog is killed painlessly and the rest is up to you.'

'Such as?'

'Oh, the casket, cremation or burial (I believe there's a waiting list for burial), a service, doggy prayers. Most of my little patients go there, in the end.'

I wondered if Turnlung knew he was living near the Dogs' Heaven. Turnlung!

I decided to keep Sally as I had made her—with human status.

'I'll phone another vet,' I called to Lenore who was in the bedroom with Sally.

'It's no use Talbot darling, she's dead.'

I went to the bedroom. Although Lenore was not crying she appeared to be close to tears and almost in a state of shock.

'She's dead. She's the only link you and I had with each other, Talbot.'

I was bewildered. From the way she spoke, one might have thought Sally was our child and we have been married and considering a separation but had stayed together 'for the sake of the child' who, being dead now, had at last set us free. I could not fathom how Sally had ever been a link between me and Lenore.

I'd never owned another animal, and I'd never owned anything as completely as I owned Sally. Yet so often I had seen her anaesthetised that I found myself readily accepting her apparent or real suspension of life. It was Lenore who wept, as if I had set my own valve of grief in her body, while I myself stayed dry-eyed. I carried Sally's dead weight into the sitting room and lay her in the basket that was her bed and I felt then, for the first time, the oppressive quality of death, the way death is able to come and go and leave its baggage to be dealt with by those who may not be practised forwarding agents, as the difficulty is to decide how much of the dead should be kept, how much sent on, while the innocent agent is all unaware that such decisions are made in secret by the dead only.

'What will you do with her?' Lenore asked.

'I'll take her to the hospital and they can use her for dissection.'

Lenore looked at me in silence for a few seconds. 'Isn't that cruel?'

Her glance said, Our only child!

I was abrupt. 'Of course not. I want her to keep her human status.'

Lenore flared with anger, her face growing pale. "*Human status!*'

The only times I saw Lenore really angry were when some

remark or incident touched the feeling she had about her early
life and her father's profession as a doctor within the Nazi
party. I had felt that this was one of the attractions she had
for me. Whether or not she wanted it to be so, death, through
the eyes of her father, looked out of her eyes, while a betrayal
of love, through the eyes of my grandfather gave me, too, a
deathly inheritance, and I could not have begun to discover
the subtleties of this relationship ruled by shadows that
consumed and drained and denied and patterned their
substance.

Sally lay dead in her basket. Both Lenore and I seized the
opportunity to put our love to rest there also. It could not resist
the magnetic moment of death.

I spoke coolly. 'I'd rather have Sally on the dissecting table
than in a ridiculous Dogs' Heaven.'

'But—*human status*! You said yourself that even the aborted
foetuses deserve a sanctuary in death—or was that just in the
beginning before your studies tampered with, contaminated
your life? *Our* life. And supposing you *are* giving Sally human
status, have you thought what your own status might become?'

'I suppose you mean inhuman,' I said, not caring. 'It's not
as simple as that.'

'Talbot,' Lenore said. 'You can't *hide* between statuses.'

'I wasn't trying to.'

'It seems to me as if you were.'

'I don't feel I am.'

'I think you may be.'

The argument was manageable only on the childish basis
of You are, I'm not. I could have reached out and pulled at
her long blond hair until her head tipped back and she cried
I give in, I give in. She sat down at the table set for breakfast,
the coffee already poured and growing cold, and began to drink

her coffee.

'I guess I'm starving,' I said.

She looked across at me, for we had taken the seats that the long-married take, facing each other. I thought with a chill recalling a dim fantasy of marriage, that she would report afterward to a neighbour or friend, *He wasn't able to look me in the eye.*

'Who's Turnlung?' she asked.

'Turnlung?'

'It's an unusual name. Is it a real name or a pseudonym. I spoke to him on the phone last night.'

'What did he say?'

'He sent you his love. Who is he?'

'He's an old man, a writer. He's working with me in my Death studies. The Field studies,' I said.

The name Turnlung seemed to fill the room. I felt its vulnerability. I felt that Lenore might try to destroy it. A thousand names, Turnlung, Turnlung, Turnlung, like butterflies filling the room, and Lenore's glance containing the power of a lethal spray.

'He's an old man, a writer,' I said again, trying to break the spell.

'And what are you going to do about him? Has *he* human status, like Sally?'

'He coming to live here,' I said quickly.

'As a substitute for me or for Sally?' Lenore's voice was cold and calm.

I didn't answer.

'You know it's no use,' she said. 'Why pretend?'

I looked down at Sally in her basket. I leaned over to touch her paw. It was still like a small brown branch that I picked up and let drop.

Lenore left that day, at noon. In my mind I heard myself describing her departure to Turnlung, saying. 'She left at *noon*,' placing emphasis on the word *noon*, as if it were of special significance.

She did not say goodbye to Sally and her goodbye to me was cold and formal. She left carrying her small case of possessions, as if she had merely been one of those saleswomen who, if they can persuade you to let them into your home, will sell you goods at a discount, but if you decide not to buy they will smilingly return the bottles and jars to their small salescase, close it, and calmly leave, with the confident attitude that they will perhaps make a sale elsewhere in the district. And when they leave, it is as if they had never visited you, they are so careful and clean.

I felt lonely when Lenore had gone. I wondered how I would break the news to my family. I noticed that, unlike the saleswomen, she, with her usual good taste, had left behind on the dressing table, the ring I had bought her.

Sally's deadness now filled the apartment. I listened for the subdued ticking of the clock, thinking that it may have stopped, as there was a feeling that some essential element in the apartment had ceased to function. Sally is dead, I told myself. And Lenore has gone. Suddenly I was aware of a feeling of anticipation, as if in two swift departures I had springcleaned my life. I was waiting, now for Turnlung to move in. I remembered that I had not really answered Lenore's question. 'Who is Turnlung?' The weight of death and loss made an instant transformation to lightness and where normally I would have explored this, asking why, when, how, where, what, I now felt so buoyant that I asked nothing, I merely accepted what had happened as further evidence of the deceitfulness of death and loss, where dead becomes alive, lost is found, empty is filled, and I think I understood what Turnlung had been trying to tell me in the park, that government is not by life and death but by language.

I wrapped Sally in one of her dog blankets. As I seldom used my car in the city as parking was a problem, I fitted Sally into a medium-sized suitcase, snapped the lock, and I guessed that I, too, must have resembled a salesman as I carried my suitcase downstairs into the crisp acceptably polluted day. Anyone observing the comings and goings from my apartment might have wondered at the transactions completed there but would never have known that the morning had seen, among other unnamed operations, amputation and death.

When I returned from giving Sally to my colleagues at the Pathology Laboratory I felt free to make the telephone the only other living being in the apartment. I waited for it to signal its life by ringing. I waited for Turnlung to speak.

18

Talbot Edelman once carried a sackful of brains
from Sweden to U.S.A.
We are dying to earn a living, they said,
punning softly like a dream with an undertone,
only they had no tongue and could not speak
yet some part of them was already marked out
as a zone for language, the password unknown,
as only a hint of disposal toward words,
as only the shadows of weathervanes turned by the memory
of a wind that might have blown.
They are living very happily settled
within the boundaries of Formalin,
the city which most believes in historical preservation.

Grant me ease in death.
A santuary. Benedictus.

* * *

Dear Selwyn come home to me in your torn overcoat
waving the handtowel you bought me for Christmas,
the one with the enormous rose in the middle like a blood-
    stain.
I can see your thin face and lips. You are going to complain
about the weather, you are tired of the rain, of slopping
about in the garden, squelch, in your galoshes. Selwyn,
I've a fire burning in the fireplace tonight.
Come home, sit like scissors on the hearth,
snip snap in the old way, cutting through my care,
though your lean face in the end was the face of a shark
and your eyes were ocean eyes and your teeth never let go.
Cut cut snip snap and bite deep, Selwyn, that was your motto.

* * *

I bought a waxed apple for thirty-nine cents. Eating it,
I ate Plaster of Paris. With a dislocated mouth
I talk to the world and the words come out
fractured, unset, in spite of their apple-cast.
I too was broken by the clamber and the fall, ripening
my heart out on a grassy floor
where shadows netted the world corner to corner.

Perhaps I never did suppose my wits would last.
Witan, to know. O all my knowing
has vacated the dwelling
in legal language that is not what it is.
What is dead and what is living? Is it snowing, is it sunning?
The witanagemot has folded up, apple jack will not love me,
the waxed mouthful starches the once-flexible words. Selwyn
    dear, where the young tree

135

with the black bark grows I will sit summerlong and cry
a witless nobody with my death swimming
like a tiger-fish in my eye.

The overworked woodpeckers have at last produced their
    testimony;
they were typing it all night, words in the pores of the tree-skin
drawing out the blood to nest in; let us get our keys on it
a few enticing taps will do it; let us get in and live and swim,
let us carry the evidence for the aged defendant
up and down the corridors of his blood, like banners, for he is
    mad.

At last the judge has given me custody of the buffalo.
I have promised to keep it warm, to educate it,
to teach it the American way of life,
how to procreate, shoot, shit and die; and the catechism of
    comfort,
and how to eradicate, defoliate the forest of Why.
I sit diseased in a clearing of thought
a witless nobody with my death swimming in my eye.

I am allowed noon and midnight visits to my daughter.
I may exercise her on the prairie between two and five
every third afternoon of each week of every second month
and our outings must be known officially as E.V.A.
Extravehicular activity, the vehicle being history.

I must prevent her from speaking to strangers—the grey wolf
    and the red fox.
    I must make sure she refuses the sweets of the sun
enticingly wrapped in light, and controls the impulse to turn

and follow
the all-night full moon which follows her about,
and if I teach her skilfully enough I know she will learn.

And we must never talk of the massacre, the incompatibility
between people and animals that led to war,
nor about how people wear and use her hide and horn,
for she would not understand; she might wish she had never
    been born;
the new knowledge forced unthinkingly upon her would be
a traumatic experience requiring excision by psychiatry.

All this I have promised faithfully. Talbot Edelman, my
    daughter and I
will race with the wind on the golden prairie, and follow the
    moon.

And it will not matter if the weather is sun, snow or rain, out
    there
on the edge of earth-space. Perhaps we shall learn to fly
(Talbot Edelman, my daughter and I)
and no one will ever see us again, not even the severe judge.

19

When Turnlung phoned the next day he said he had arranged for the custody of his daughter, and when I said I had not known about his daughter his reply was, 'Of course you do. It's *our* daughter, yours and mine.'

After Lenore's hint that Sally the dog had been like our child, and now Turnlung's news, I felt I was becoming a versatile father.

'Daughter buffalo.'

'Daughter buffalo?'

'Yes. Remember her? It's all arranged. She need not stay there. They have given me custody of her, with many rights and privileges and responsibilities, as,' he added slyly, 'in our language these are grouped together. Do you want me to list them?'

I said 'no' uncertainly.

'I've written them down. You may read them later,' he said.

I was not completely bewildered. When all other doors are barred, the door into and out of fantasy is forever open and it was good for an old man in whose house the furniture was being gradually removed, the doors locked, shutters put up, drapes pulled down, to find a place which the furniture removers had not invaded.

'Did you recover,' I asked, 'from the spell in Central Park?'

'I've been taking it easy; going slowly; in my room writing my death notes, with all the dead returning to me, yet never with their deaths. Oh, no, you don't suppose the dead will give their *death* away—only with their lives. It seems to me that the best way to hold on to life is to die. And what about us, Talbot?'

I had a memory then like a sad compelling dream of a house and furniture and high ceilings, of childhood and warmth both dry and wet warmth, and weeping, as small boys do when they are lost among the wares in a supermarket or standing on a street corner, howling and howling, their mouths wide, emptying their hearts of a primitive sorrow that only partly belongs to them and does not ask to be understood.

'Can you visit me here?' I said. 'Take a cab. I'll pay.' I wondered if he had thought over my impulsive invitation to stay. I hoped he had forgotten it. I was appalled by my hypocrisy yet I kept saying to myself, This is no place for him. There must be somewhere for him to go. He can't stay here. Not with me.

An hour later Turnlung rang my doorbell, identifying himself through the entry phone. I began unlocking the several locks on my apartment door, finally slipping the chain free and opening the door. I could hear him walking slowly up the stone steps, stopping at each landing to get his breath. A tall goblet-shaped ashtray filled with sand stood just outside the door and in it, among the cigarette butts a dead cockroach lay on its back with its legs in the air. I glared at it, my irritation with the increasing discomfort and noise of the apartment con-

centrating itself upon this cockroach, the first I had seen in
the building. I could hear the tenants of the apartment next
to mine talking loudly in their German, making conversations
that always sounded like quarrels, whether they were dining
or entertaining or sincerely arguing or in the midst of their
audible love-making. The two with their unboundaried
presence occupied every apartment adjoining theirs, and I felt
they should have paid some of my rent. They not only insisted
with their living and loving dialogue, on entering my
apartment, they allowed the smoke and smell from their potent
cigarettes and cigars to seep under the partition wall while at
each of their meals and at every bathroom visit I was con-
scripted to share their accompanying smells.

Turnlung reached the landing.

'My footsteps echo,' he said. 'It's dark on the stairway.'

'One of the light bulbs has gone,' I said. 'When something
breaks down here there isn't a hope of its being repaired or
replaced.'

'But you don't have to live here, do you? Didn't you say you
could find somewhere else? Somewhere...cleaner.'

Turnlung hesitated over the word. Over our lunch in the
Natural History Museum I had told him almost everything
about myself.

'But how are you, my dear?'

He embraced me and kissed me, on the cheek this time, like
a brother—the word *comrade* came to mind, so clearly
describing friendship and love between men: a warm
encompassing word. Comrades, in one's imagination, wore
heavy overcoats to keep out the cold world of snow and ice,
and their faces glowed with love for each other as their bodies
hurried to distribute the restless blood where it was most
needed, all in a warm protective transport beyond the intru-

sion of harsh outward weather with its shrillness, in its unforeseen arrivals and departures and its imposition of differences: the comrades in their greatcoats, in their one greatcoat, together, were a mirror image of each other, affirming each other, a perfect exchange of shadow and substance.

As soon as Turnlung came beyond the small entrance hall he frowned, sensing the recent activity and the emptiness of the apartment.

'There's been a death. What's happened?'

'Lenore,' I said.

Turnlung looked startled. 'Dead?'

'Oh no.'

I realised then that I had never imagined or feared her death, therefore, if further proof were needed, I had never loved her, for the gift which comes with love is the special fear of the death of the beloved, the preoccupation with it, waking and dreaming, the relentless working out of the subtraction sum and its horrifying answer.

'No,' I said. 'Sally died. I miss her. She was a diseased but living part of myself. I had changed her, broken her bones, multilated her, transplanted her, stolen half her quota of breath by collapsing one lung. I did everything to her, except make love. I even removed her ovaries. I tampered with her. That's the word. Tampered, made corrupting changes.'

Turnlung seized the word. 'Tamper. Tamper. A well-tempered dog. You merely tuned her toward her death. But you also mutilated her.'

'I had to. She was my work.'

'And you never made love to her?'

'One does have fantasies, at times, of penetrating, not always in the habitual places.'

Turnlung echoed my words. 'One does have fantasies. What did she die of?'

'Some internal infection, not an ordinary dog disease. Probably delayed complications of her most recent surgery.'

'So you gave her a human death?'

'You could say that.'

'What about Lenore? What death did you choose for her? What did you remove from her?'

I had noticed Turnlung's habit of merciless questioning. He did not seem to care what feelings he roused in me.

'What did you remove from Lenore?' he repeated.

'Something which I found I'd never given her but which both she and I believed she had. Therefore I performed phantom surgery to remove it.'

'Smart boy,' he said, a little sarcastically. 'So now you're free?'

'I expect I am.'

'When will you finish your death studies?'

'Quite soon, sooner than I think.'

We'd been walking restlessly up and down the big studio-sitting room, walking into the bedroom, the bathroom, the kitchen, as if the apartment were a cage, for our pace was rapid, in step, and urgent, and our heads were thrust forward. As we talked and I glanced at Turnlung I saw that his face was paler than usual, and I forgave him his questions; our quick pace and urgency made the questions belong to the language of the imprisoned where little but the personal is of any concern. Even his question, 'So now you're free?' emphasised the reality of the cage.

I suggested we sit near the window. I pointed out the trees newly in leaf but I could see that Turnlung's attention was straying.

He stared out of the window. 'Oh? The trees?' he said,

seeming not to understand.

There was a harassed look in his eyes. The grey strands of his hair lay untidily over his forehead and he kept brushing his hand distractedly across his face and eyes, as if to clear his view.

I feared the conclusions I drew from his appearance for, in the geriatric patients, it was the outward appearance which gave evidence of inner dishevelment, often of incipient senile psychosis. We sat facing each other. I felt as if I were at my first homecoming in a life of human vagrancy. I was of the generation which expected to receive more than it gave. I had been brought up to know abundance. The word 'without' was not often used by me or members of my family. Turnlung, I felt, had been carrying my life, entrusted with it in an unfamiliar land all these years while I, in my native land, tried to learn the language of the life imposed upon me. He was the jeweller (did he not say the word 'jewel' was set in the centre of his life?) who makes a long difficult journey to bring the genuine stone to one who had been deceived in his life not only by an imitation jewel but by a genuine imitation. He had given me the jewel and I had accepted it as naturally as I accepted gifts all my life. I had taken what I wanted from Sally and from Lenore. I did not consider the nature of the bereavement which Turnlung might suffer. I had no plans then, to remove his heart, brain or lungs.

What followed was an act of recognition between us. Turnlung, naked, brought a detachment over me as if I returned to the hospital wards where the rows of old men lay all alike in the state of their skin and flesh and bone, their helplessness, their querulous voices spotted with saliva. I felt hate rising in me against Turnlung. And against myself. We became briefly two-dimensional, images only, in mirrors; the old and the young Narcissus. I who have never known poverty in the usual sense felt hate for his life and my life and the apparently generous yet insufficient ration of bodily parts issued to us. We were ingenious as man and man must be, but 'making do' had always been the admired occupation of others, of those who lived in the poorer places, who were admonished by their parents,

Use it up,
wear it out,
make it do
or do without,

a rhyme which had once brought to my innocent mind an image of sweaters being worn to the last thread, bread eaten to the last crust and crumb.

At first, then, I hated Turnlung and myself, revealing my hate in cruelty. And finally I felt love and gratitude, given and taken as a reward, and a sense of safety and shelter which I had never known with Lenore with whom I had felt trapped, unable to retreat. With Turnlung I felt protected by one whose body was in my own image though aged and much used, so that what I felt for him I also felt for myself; he gave me permssion to mourn and rejoice over my own life. I was using Turnlung. I felt like a child whose father opens a closet to show the suit the child might wear when he is an old man; and when the father has left the room the child takes the suit and tries it on and walks up and down in front of the mirror saying, within the enormity of his idea of time, 'This is me in two hundred years,' contorting his face to his imagination and knowledge of how an old man's face may be, bending his back, his knees, quavering his voice.

Our act was a rehearsal of time—for me, of the future, for Turnlung of the past. We made love to our own lives and deaths.

'I'm too old for it,' Turnlung said. A bewildered look came into his face. 'What do you think my daughter would say? *Our* daughter?'

I was not then thinking of our daughter. I was secretly hoping that Turnlung would become bedridden, that I would attend to all his physical needs. He would stay in my apartment. I would remain home, looking after him. And when he died, as he must do soon, I thought, I would be at his deathbed to comfort and farewell him, seeing him safely into the sanctuary.

It was a dream I had, I knew there was no place for Turnlung in my apartment or in my life.

The afternoon had almost gone. We sat by the window again, silently looking out at the trees and the garden below. The sky was darkening, its underside growing a coat of dull fur, the accumulated deposits of breath and fumes lining the city as if it were an old cooking vessel.

'By the way,' Turnlung said. 'About your invitation to stay . . .'

I interrupted quickly. 'I find it can't be managed. I wish I could, but there's no place here in this apartment. I'm sure you'll agree.'

'My dear . . .'

He looked hurt. Then he said, with a gesture of his hand brushing his mouth as if to tidy up a few stray feelings, some of love, some of bewilderment, 'I suppose you're right. I'm okay now, right as rain. That spell in the park is over. But there's Daughter Buffalo. . . And us.'

He was like a young lover rushing into the first-person plural on the slightest excuse. I felt that I preferred to remain in the first-person singular. I shut my eyes to try to rid myself of the reality of the dream of him.

'You mean our daughter in the zoo?' I said.

'I now have custody of her,' he said. 'I told you? With your apartment being so close to Central Park, I thought I'd like to accept your invitation to stay. We could go together to visit our daughter.' Then he reached out to me and plucked at my sleeve as if I were a passerby and he were a beggar desperate for a morsel of information, 'Which country are we in? Are your parents still living?'

When the old grow suddenly senile (senility in medical terms means merely old age; I am speaking of the popular usage, senility as mental decay. I could use the geological meaning: approaching a period of erosion) there is within a short time a house- or mind-cleaning of gigantic proportions where almost every thought and memory are discarded. I have always been fascinated by what is retained and why it is chosen or chooses itself. A woman may remember only her husband's name. If he is alive she may no longer recognise him, looking on him only as 'a nice kind man living in this house with me'. She might say, 'My husband Harry would be glad I have this nice man living with me.' Often the mind refuses to part with stock sentences—'Have you had a good journey?' 'Are your parents living?' 'Do you often visit this part of the world?'— where the aged compile a tourist phrase book for their own use in their own country which is now foreign to them. 'Do the trains still pass this way?' 'Are the buses running?' 'I would like to get in touch with the Ambassador.' A conversation may be like that of Rosencrantz and Guildenstern:

'The weather is good.'

'Yes the weather is good.'

'But cold.'

'Very cold.'

'It's warm at night.'

'Much warmer, much warmer.'

And if you put the senile among those with memory you watch them struggling as in a foreign land to interpret what is being said around them.

I knew that such changes had come over my grandfather. Seeing the first evidence in Turnlung of an end to memory I wondered to what extent our love had applied the finishing touch. As a sun, with the blessings of a sun, it may have matured the seeds of senility which could neither help their blossoming nor reverse their growth. I knew that for Turnlung to be denied clear seeing at the end of his life was like being sentenced to living death, and yet I felt that perhaps he had known what would happen and—this thought suddenly removed from me my feelings of safety—he had steered himself toward me, sensing that he could survive by emptying his life into mine. I felt afraid. I understood now why my mother had refused hospitality to my grandfather, though I did not forgive her refusal, and I did not forgive my own when I heard myself making it.

'There must be some place you can go,' I said. 'I mean there are many places which cater...'

He interrupted. 'I don't like the word 'cater'. You know how I am with words, Talbot dear. I get so annoyed with them. 'Cater' is not a word for me. I'm not trading my life or my death. What about Daughter Buffalo? She will need proper training and education and a little language will do her no harm; a word here, a word there; a planet or star or two above the prairie; and I, Turnlung, say that she shall not be tricked or threatened by words but she will race with the wind toward them, and trust them, and know the promises they give and those they withhold, and never confuse them with the promises she may make to herself.

'What do you think of that, Talbot? Your name is Talbot Edelman?'

'My name is Talbot Edelman.'

'I look on it as a miracle.'

I affirmed that it was a miracle.

'It's time I went home now,' Turnlung said. 'I have much to do. How long is it since our walk through Reptile Hall? I hope you say the prayer each night.'

His memory had not entirely failed. I heard him say, *testitudines crocodylia rhynchocephalia, squamata, sauria, serpentes*...

Down in the street I found a cab for Turnlung, put him in it, paid the driver, and asked that Turnlung be delivered, like a parcel, to the exact address, right inside the door of his apartment house. Then I went upstairs where I cleaned the bathroom and removed all trace of Turnlung from the bedroom and the sitting room.

'I am not a family man,' I kept saying to myself.

It appeared that the first choice fantasy of Turnlung's approaching senility was his being part of the family group from which he had always been an outcast. Yet had he?

I remembered his prayer for living things, *squamata, sauria, serpentes*...

Grandfather was an outcast, too, I told myself. I felt that I had failed Grandfather and Turnlung and myself. My senility was being experienced in geological meaning. I too was suffering a form of erosion.

20

A week later, breaking my lease, I moved out of my apartment onto the sixteenth floor of a building overlooking Central Park South where I surrounded myself once again with warmth and comfort and 'taste'—my pre-Columbian art. Here there was no raw wood resembling coffin wood; all surfaces were finished and stained and polished, subjected to the conventional treatment for corpses and wood. I felt at home. I felt safe from Turnlung. I could not imagine him in my new home; he was raw, foreign, his accent was uncut, he was from a land which had not yet been glazed with people, where the rivers were only then being 'tamed' to obedience to the hydro-electric impulse or reflex; where the children's playgounds were not yet paved with plastic turf, where clay, not plastic foam, touched the flesh feet standing on the real earth. An unfinished land. Why, even the native peoples had not been 'finished' in the way we have finished ours! Turnlung, I thought, would not fit into my controlled environment, just as our grandfather had not fitted into the home and life of our family.

I had not heard from Turnlung. I decided to wait until the

after-shocks of our last meeting had quietened, and I had settled once again into my American way of life, and as I was an instant settler in an instant world I planned to get in touch with him within a few days. I worried about him. There must be a place for him, I told myself. I knew from my experience with the aged that they may wake one morning with all their normal mental functioning dislocated and their sense of time and place gone, and I suspected, from Turnlung's temporary states of disorientation that he too might wake one morning soon, knowing nothing and needing nursing care, as if he were an infant. The stress of much travel, the changes of age, the demands of loving, the new responsibilities put upon him by his new 'family'—these, I felt, were leading him to a final confusion, yet not entirely unhappily; his new family was a shining satisfaction for him and it would be a treasured stepping-stone by which he could make a dignified path to unreason. He was managing very well, I thought, in putting the finishing touches to his mind. His loss would be his profit. His mind would become, as they say, 'an empty shell'.

The trend of my thoughts horrified me. I saw myself using Turnlung as shells are used to re-create echoes of distant time and place, recent love and sadness, departures, vacancies, all heard and relived through the sound and rhythm of the washing in and out of tides of blood. He would become a personal echo of greetings, goodbyes, and though all in him would appear to be lost, nothing would be lost; his universal echo would be heard in cathedrals—he would *become* a cathedral, a mountaintop. a crossroad and cross of bone; he would be used completely.

This point of use was our meeting place: artist and scientist both sitting down at the feast of use. Brought up in my material world of no deposit no return, of collapsible disposable containers and goods, seeing the infection of disposability spreading to humankind which could be discarded along with beer cans and paper plates and cups and wooden ice-cream spoons, I was beginning to learn from the so-called 'disposables' themselves, that use is indestructible and eternal. The commonplace credit cards that defied disintegration, the detergent and bleach bottles, put safely out of sight and mind, which reappeared buoyantly riding the seas of the world, strewn with the seaweed and the shells on faraway coasts, the DDT in the lichen of the far north and in the penguin fat of the far south—these reminded me that nothing is ever lost or unworthy of use. I may have been brought up in a world where both the animate and the inanimate are disposable, yet I had some feeling about the lethal and the life-giving deposits left by individual people and by nations. I valued the traces of my grandfather and of Turnlung. I promised myself that although I could not offer Turnlung a home, I could make sure that he did not become lost among the so-called 'disposables', that whatever his condition he would be recognised as human, and used, even to an extremity of use which might parallel our recent loving, by there being so little to use.

21

I decided that after I had given my family the news about Lenore I would again get in touch with Turnlung.

I called Mother, inviting her to tea in the new apartment. She was delighted, she said. She would combine her visit with shopping for Lenore and me, and Daddy would come with her and drive her home, as it would be his weekly gallery visit. My usual paralysis of will prevented me from telling her at once that Lenore and I had separated. I had no intention of talking to her about my sexual preferences, by way of explanation, for to me sex was a private style which two people discovered to be satisfying, like a brand of toothpaste of a size of shirt. In my work I'd met a variety of attitudes and philosophies and I knew that at least one of my colleagues had begun a practical exploration of rape as the only form of sex to give satisfaction to both participants. Others indulged in spectator sex, so sophisticated that the description of it could not be encompassed by the archaic countrified picture of 'Peeping Tom'. In my clinic I had many opportunities to explore the dead sexually but I had little interest in this, believing there were enough of the living dead who might consent to provide satisfaction.

Therefore, though my mother might not have thought so, my attraction for Turnlung was 'homely' in the complete sense of the word; it had been derived in part from my experience of 'home', from the memory or image of my faceless bodiless grandfather who had no place in the family; and it may not have been derived in some way from the home comforts of non-death where the rich upholstery of the furniture, the plump cushions, the deep carpets were to be used and respected but never stained, and where the four bathrooms in a house of four people existed to clean the people thoroughly, making them spotless with non-death.

I was apprehensive about Mother's visit. I was glad that Father would be there, focusing attention on his new painting while I quietly gave my news. They would arrive, inspect the apartment, have tea or coffee, show me the painting, and somewhere between these activities I would insert lightly, or, if leverage were necessary, determinedly,

'Lenore and I have separated. We're not marrying.'

Or,

'Lenore and I have cancelled our wedding.'

My mother would reply,

'Cancelled? You mean *postponed*.'

'No. Cancelled.'

'But that's impossible. How do you mean, cancelled?'

Lenore and I have separated, I thought, might sound less startling than cancelled. (I felt suddenly lonely for Turnlung and the sly remarks he would make about these alternative ways of telling one truth.)

Finally, I rehearsed until I could say it smoothly in one breath: 'Lenore and I have agreed to separate. We're not getting married after all.'

Saturday was smoky, polluted, and at midmorning it began to rain a tropical downpour from a storm lurking off the East Coast on its way to Nantucket. People in the streets ran in the rain-panic that overcomes those in the cities, cowering from the torrents of oil- and litter-filled water flung at them by lurching cabs and buses, while the vents in the street hissed their suddenly active hell-steam in hot wet spirals, all in a rain so remote from its original blessing that the people might have been forgiven for having the look of the damned in being forced to bear the meaninglessness and inconvenience of city weather. I looked out of my window at the darkened city with its lights already burning at midday and the pall of unbreathable air breaking and sliding down the rain into millions of lung-closets beneath. Now and then lightning split the sky, scissoring the seams of the pall which closed together after it had passed, invisibly stitched by the thread trailing from incinerator and factory chimneys and car and plane exhausts.

My parents arrived complaining, out of the storm. Rain in the city, Mother said, was so useless. My father carried the painting he had bought, holding it protectively.

'Is Lenore here?' Mother asked as I draped their wet coats on the hangers.

'I knew that other apartment wasn't right for you,' she said, without waiting for an answer, and glancing with approval at the sitting room and into the bathroom. 'This is what we imagined for you when you first came to New York—remember, when you first wanted to rent a place here? We used to talk about it at night, your daddy and I, and we'd plan it for you, and this is how it was, just as you have it now. Oh,' she said, crying out at the sight of long-lost friends, 'your pre-Columbian pieces! But where's Lenore?'

'Lenore? She's not here.'

Then I began to speak loudly because I didn't want to have to repeat my news, I wanted it to be understood clearly and immediately.

'Lenore and I have cancelled our wedding. We've parted.'

I had not known I would get so much pleasure from saying the world *cancelled*. I was glad that I had used it.

Mother repeated it as if she too were fascinated by its finality and richness and its use in all the important transactions of living and dying, and the memories accompanying it, of lost childhood parties and games, of rain and storm, of irretrievable letters and numbers, and obliterated dreams and lives.

'Cancelled?'

'Yes.'

'You mean you don't love each other? But of course you do.'

My father was looking shocked but more uncertain.

'If he says they don't love each other then they don't.' He looked at me for confirmation. 'Do you?'

'No. We've agreed.'

Mother's feelings were still arrested at the word 'cancelled'.

'Cancelled,' she said again. 'My poor baby.'

I knew this reaction to be false as she had never felt me to be her baby. The garbage disposal unit had been her only baby. I accepted the falseness, however, for I'd long learned that the daily average sincerity count between person and person is low and must be compensated for by a number of other qualities which have higher readings.

'We wanted to see you with a wife and family,' Mother said kissing me gently on my cheek. 'Lenore was a nice girl.'

Infected by Mother's use of the past tense my father said, 'Yes, she was a nice girl. We'll miss her.'

'She's accepted that offer in Germany,' I said. 'At the clinic. She has already left, she flew the other day.'

I had removed her both in space and time.

My father frowned, thinking of Germany. Then he remembered his painting.

'I must show you my painting. It's a seascape by an unknown. They tried to make me buy something more fashionable but I said this was modern enough for me.'

Seeming to forget the tea, the cancelled wedding, my father unwrapped the painting and propped it up on a coffee table near the window to get both the light from the standard lamp and the meagre light from the gloomy sky.

'But you look right over Central Park,' Mother exclaimed in the persuasive tone I remembered she had used when speaking of Grandfather in the nursing home: 'He has such a wonderful view of the woods in all seasons!'

She beckoned to my father, adjusting the painting. 'See, he looks right over Central Park. You'll be able to walk that dog of yours, Sally, the poor creature. What have you done with her?'

'She died.'

'I'm not going to grieve,' Mother said. 'I'm sure she welcomed her death. There's something in you, Talbot, that I can't understand, the way you made that dog, your pet, suffer; and still you removed her organs, took out her eye; and all those experiments you performed on her heart!'

'The dog heart is very close to the human heart, Mother,' I reminded her. 'And she did enjoy life, Mother. She had the trees and the sun when it shone, and the view.'

Mother looked puzzled. 'The view? And now there's this business with Lenore. What happened between you two?'

My father was waiting patiently for our attention. Without

answering my mother I stood back to study the painting. It was Father's usual seascape, for he himself was an artist in that, as artists may paint the same painting all their lives, so my father certainly bought the same painting: sea or landscape with or without people; untroubled sun and sky, or a storm that was in no danger of being projected into the 'real' world, so safely was it locked within the frame of its canvas. Father did not develop in his choice of painting. His last would be his first as he needed the recognition which he could give to them and which they gave to him. One glance at a painting and he knew it was his 'kind'; and we knew also, and often, seeing one of 'father's paintings' in a place miles from Madison Avenue we would be tempted to buy it for him, as one might buy postage stamps for a special collection of one design.

I had long ago guessed that the paintings were Father's sure 'place', so abiding that the fluid light and water and land might have been composed of stone. This necessity for sanctuary so clearly felt by my open-hearted generous father always moved me by its hint of darkness in a nature which was supposedly full of light. I thought, at times, that I should have replaced all my ideas about my father with new feelings which would make him almost unrecognisable to me, that somewhere in my early life I had used the wrong emotional vehicle on the wrong path in my childhood journey to what I thought was his nature and being. It became hard to turn back; I panicked at the thought of beginning again; it was easier to continue, with mistaken ideas and feelings woven into the truth.

'Oh. Ah,' Mother exclaimed loyally as at last we studied the painting. 'It's beautiful.'

She spoke sincerely. She thought all his paintings were beautiful, though she criticised him for not assessing, as others did, the 'true market value', and thus for not having made a fortune from resale, and when Father countered this by reminding her that he consistently bought the work of unknown painters, Mother replied by asking how was it that the unknowns bought by others so readily became the 'knowns'. She did not nag about it, however. She came from a business family and she liked to see the business sense in operation in all walks of life. When I had told her of my ambition to be a doctor, although she welcomed the humanitarian nature of my work, she at once performed a pleasing calculation of my likely income.

'The painting really is beautiful.' My father flushed with delight.

'I like it too,' I said, with an absurd need to rival my mother in her approval.

It was a beach scene, in acrylic, yet if one half-closed one's eyes one had the illusion that the waves were grass, the waters a prairie. The flecked waves stopped at midripple, the bathers like blades of green and blue light, unnaturally elongated, slashed the water in midleap; the sky was vast and pale blue with clouds layered in a white that was like the colour of sickness—the clouds looks 'unwell'. In the foreground, on the sand, with its back to the ocean and the bathers, a small white dog stood, its pose and expression introducing (with the 'sick clouds) the only other element of unpleasantness. The dog's face was full of hurt and furious rage, almost a human rage. The name of the painting was Noon. It was high noon, vividly the moment when the vertical sun strikes. No object portrayed had a shadow. I could feel the heat on the top of my head as Turnlung and I had felt the sun that day in Central Park.

I began to sweat in the heat. I felt that I could not escape from the painting, from the furious dog caught in the shafts of sun, from the bathers fixed and speared by the fire, from the dog's evident rage against noon, against the time of most quiet and lassitude and helplessness when the sun attaches lead weights to all parts of the body and the swift-running shadows of man and beast are cancelled, or shrunk to the size of small breakfast plates broken or stacked out of sight of the earth; it is the moment of disbelief in substance and self when light, the liquid paradigm, would persuade all substance to melt and flow into the sky, yet at the same time would anchor all beneath its mass of heat. The opposing impulses, I thought, showed clearly in the small white dog which appeared as a kind of human representative, raging because he could not melt and fly, raging because he could not become stone.

I had never studied one of my father's paintings so intently and intensely, chiefly, I supposed, because I had little need to. Now, out of my recent experience, my meeting with Turnlung, my obsession with him and my longing to free myself from him, Sally's death, my parting with Lenore, and the intuitive knowledge of death which was being transmitted to me, not only in the field studies but through my own loving and parting and loss, and my guilt, and the presence of my grandfather, I had an intensity to bestow where it would be received and absorbed and would not alarm with the accompanying demand that I show responsibility for it.

'Yes, I like the painting very much,' I said.

I was shivering. I half-closed my eyes and saw the waves as · grass of a prairie. The palms of my hands were damp with sweat.

'I knew you'd like it. It's a fine piece of work.'

He pointed to it in the manner of a teacher giving a lesson. 'See the sea, those waves, that vastness?'

Mother and I nodded to say, yes, we saw the vast sea and the waves.

'And the dog. Right in the middle, the dog.'

'Yes.'

'And the bathers.'

'Oh yes.'

'And look at the sky. Just look at that blue.'

'Oh yes, the blue.'

'And just look at that milky green of the waves, the sharper blues. What exquisite colours.'

'Oh yes, that green.'

And the dog again. Those eyes. That face.

'Yes. The dog.'

'I don't expect you to answer this, but have you ever seen such a peaceful noon setting, not a trace of unpleasantness, that little dog there full of the delights of being alive, the joy of being on the sand near the water; those bathers cool against the hot sun?'

'They haven't any faces,' my mother said, as a remark, not a criticism.

'Faceless bathers,' Father said with an air of satisfaction. 'Faceless' was a word he had used much in the past two years after having come across it somewhere in a way that was significant to him. Carefully he began to return the painting to its package. He kept saying, 'I knew you'd like it.'

They sat, no doubt musing on the pleasantness and the little successes of life—the happy choice of paintings, books, music, guests, presents, the attractiveness of weather in its right place, among trees and lakes and under skies, the dryness of dry clothes in a rainy city, the gratification of having one son a successful businessman, the other a doctor, distinguished-looking, a real gentleman to his parents but not married yet.

When I had served the coffee cake Mother asked how she should go about telling the family about Lenore and me, and

I told her that we had signed a notice to appear the next day in the *Times*.

'You put it discreetly?'

I assured her I had, and that as Lenore was already in Germany she would not be worried by tactless questions.

'That beautiful ring, too! She returned it to you?'

'Yes.'

During this commonplace exchange I was doing my best to deal with the many unspoken questions while I could see that Mother was torn between her misery at the loss of a *married* son and her gratitude at having her unmarried son restored to her, though I could tell that by the time my parents were about to leave it was my mother's misery which prevailed. I think she found it impossible to dissolve the mass of family fantasy which had built itself up in her mind, grandchild by grandchild.

After tea, she washed the dishes. Lately, visiting my apartment, she had controlled her impulse to enter my kitchen as she felt it belonged now to Lenore. This day, however, she walked freely through the apartment.

'It's just like home,' she called from the kitchen. She noted that I should fill my cookie jars, which, knowing my mother, I understood to mean, not that she would bake cookies for me but that she would go to the food department of one of the big stores and have them send me an extravagantly beribboned box of assorted cookies.

'Wait,' my father said, as they were leaving. 'Here.'

He gave me the painting in its package. 'I think you could use this for that gap over the sofa, don't you? It would just fit that gap.'

He hesitated. 'You *do* like the painting?'

'Yes, yes.'

'Take it then. It's yours. Hang it in that space over there. You'll enjoy looking at it. It's hard luck that you and Lenore have broken up. A sad thing to happen.'

'Yes,' Mother said, coming forward with the coats. 'Just at this point in your career, too.'

I felt that my father was giving me the painting as a consolation prize and I think I resented the way my parents had so quickly taken over my apartment, lacking Sally and Lenore to keep them out, that they already commandeered the walls and had decided which was welcome and which was unwelcome space, like real estate dealers looking over vacant plots and planning where to build.

As if my father had read my thoughts he said, in an obstinate way, as they went out. 'Don't forget to hang the painting just in the gap above the sofa. It will give you good cheer, that painting.'

I saw my parents into the elevator and down to the street.

'It's so lovely having the view over Central Park,' Mother said.

Then down in the lobby where my father went to inspect a picture on the far wall, she said. 'What was it Talbot, between you and Lenore? I'd understand it better if you said you have quarrelled.'

'No, we didn't quarrel,' I said. 'We're still quite good friends.'

She looked horrifed. 'Good *friends*?'

'Like sister and brother,' I said, letting her deal with her conclusions in her own way.

We went out to the street. It had stopped raining. I walked with my parents the four blocks to their parked car. I thought my father looked sad without his painting-prop. I could not tell what my mother was feeling.

When I returned to my apartment I felt a sense of relief

that I had somehow rid my life of all people and animals except Turnlung.

PART FOUR

MAN, DOG, BUFFALO, DO YOU KNOW YOUR NAME?

22

How pleased I am to have found in the world's second most
        populated city
roasting or freezing on the population gridiron
two animals from which I shall construct a loving family,
which are already part of my blood. I grow maple, birch,
        hemlock,
lion-desert, all on a chemical bank with wild time, with the
        buffalo and Talbot Edelman
of the immigrant tongue, whose ancestry still occupies through
        force of history
the troubled land of aspirate, a breathing outpost of hope.

We three stand posing for our sun-photographs
against the glacial rock in Central Park.
I will send the photograph home. I will say
Here I am, here I am with my loving family
standing on the skeleton of the earth, a relic of that remote
time when the earth wore ice as an aeon overcoat
before the sun so hot so hot came out
and the earth began to sweat

and there was the first noon; and Move over, Seas, the Earth
  said,
while I take off my coat
while I hang it on the north pole and start work, cleaning up
  the place
with its litter of glaciers, discarded remnants of ice.

There are some in the universe among the planets and stars
and on the earth who lead a useful obedient working life,
not too cut up about anything, for what you don't know you
  don't miss,
and the valley of the shadow is a comfortable sheltered place
until some outsider starts to call it an abyss;
and musical echoes are the chief joy of an empty vessel
until the complaint goes out, It's empty. Why isn't it full?

I live in a room on Thirty-fourth Street, New York.
I have recorded one by one my classes in Death Education.
I think of the small absences—Mother has gone from my
  range of vision,
Father has gone from the room but I hear
their voice and their noise, and their bulk ships air
my way, and they stop the light.

And I think of the small absences from memory:
I did not think of you once today.
You did not occupy my mind.
Memories are experienced travellers, they think nothing of
  having breakfast in life
supper in death on a round trip or one way;
they do not despise luxury

and throughout man's history
they have lived within sound of the blood-sea.

Dear Aunt Kate,
You were too late to be loved,
while Uncle Dick from his grave reached forth
a mouldy tentacle into your memory,
and on the third last day of your life, your eyes, declared
    obsolete,
were put to the back of their socket-shelf,
labelled Old Stock,
Not Wanted on voyage.
Dear Aunt Kate, dear country girl born many years ago,
dead in full possession of all your Central Otago sky.

Aunt Kate, here in New York City I think of your relevant
    lilac leaves,
the heart-shaped witnesses of the fifth month;
    the easily crumpled leaves,
one thirst too much, one too swift glance of sun and they
    wither and die.

Hello silkworms plaiting a blanket for me to sleep in,
hello public feast of silk,
wormy breasts with a spout of gold milk,
what gossamer nourishment to hold up to the light before you
    die.
Your life, your life work and your death impress me—
a triumph of planning, of political economy, except for one
    item of the inventory
—the moth wings ornamental only
or so we say who become impatient if we are unable to read
    the immediate reason

(e.g. our useless appendix and third eye)
but I myself have always believed everything is for use
not necessarily by those who possess it.
I had, once, a loan of sight for my third eye.
And in summer, when the sun comes out,
I rent a tail attached to my obsolete tail-bone
and I wag my tail in enjoyment of the sun.
Also, I had new wings on loan, which I returned to the
     company
when I lost the impulse to fly.

Heterodon Platyrhynos who plays dead.

I drink *Grava* that tastes of small gritty strawberries and
     gliding grapes
which the tongue undresses, discarding the skin
which hangs on a twig to dry like any wet outerwear of man
     or fruit.
Grapes of course are invertebrate.
Within, they are a dark pool, 'wine-dark' as described by
     Homer writing of the Grecian seas
with the innumerable seed-islands
their dark-blue skin of sky.

Talbot Edelman admired my *Grava*. That day in my room
when the immortelles long dead began to bloom
and we were left in this heraldic summer
to our own devices.

I name the places: Lincoln Centre, Reptile Hall, the Buffalo
     Enclosure,
perhaps the Public Transport Authority Terminal

where the deaf and dumb distribute the cards of their alphabet
to all who wait for the Boston bus
who are shocked to read on the card they have so happily,
    freely accepted,
A small contribution please.
having the language on their tongue, families of decibels in
    their ears,
having tongue, teeth, lips, throat, ears that work
at interpretive work they are suddenly afraid of the future
    for their
tongue and ears
of being alone in a language without words.
Therfore they pay up their dollars and dimes
and, cleansed, rescued from the perils of tongueless times,
they travel to Boston where the Charles River flows
and the once-new world is old world
with cobbles and commons and crochet
and concerts and crooks and curfews.

Lately I went to the Registrar of Births and Deaths to register
    my daughter.
A notice on the wall said, *Closed*. Open tomorrow between
    ten and five.
Dear Daughter Buffalo, I said, You are not yet officially alive.
What would you like to do with your spare time until
    tomorrow?
Teach me, she said, about the prairie. So I taught her.
Talbot and I have an educable daughter.

How fine it is to be born whole, able to walk and run,
kick hooves in the air, stay unsunburned in the sun,
wear drip-dry brown fur!

I love my daughter.
I was impatient to take her to the Registrar.

We walked down Fifth Avenue. People mistook us for an
    old man and his living poster,
one of those who use babies as banners to wave against war.
They said to me, Go home, protester.
And to my daughter, Get lost, long-hair!
Let us go, dear ruminant, I said,
leading her proudly downtown.

They gave me a form to sign
to prove that she was mine.
They said, Write down the name of each parent
the age occupation and present address.
Daughter buffalo said, Grandfather died choking with a
    peanut in his windpipe,
or was it a slice of glass-filled New York angel cake?
His present address is the sky. He gallops round and round the
    sky,
his hooves knocking on the stars and planets,
his horns carrying the weightless clouds.
As for grandmothers and mothers and fathers. . .she looked
    shy.
Tell them, Dad, she said.
About him and you and me.
About Us. And why.

Surname Buffalo. Unemployed. Address Central Park Zoo.
    Zip Code?
Former residence Prairie. Daughter Buffalo.
What about Gloria, Abigail, Marily, Mae with an 'e',
Harriet or Jane, Florence or Flo,

172

there's a limitless choice you know,
the clerk said. Why just *Daughter Buffalo?*
Some parents, he muttered, have no imagination.
I paid my fee and went home
thinking how difficult it was to give birth to a buffalo
vicariously through the womb of history
among the bullboys of the Wild West.

A daughter, they used to say, is often the apple of her father's
    eye.
Meaning, her father finds her desirable and rosy-ripe enough
    to eat.
As father of a buffalo, I am more discreet.
She is my jewel. The word has come into its own at last. She is
    my death-jewel,
beauteous, and when she dies she will die a complete death,
    like a true animal
lying upon the prairie,
an instrument tuned by the wind, snow and sun
played on by the hooves of the oldest galloping stars.
I doubt if the music will fall on human ears.
I shall hear it some place in my city heart, at night, when
    Talbot Edelman and I sit warming ourselves by our central
    heat,
sleepy and fifty percent inert.

Heterodon Platyrhinos who plays dead.

(The furred bees dancing at the door of the flowering currant,
the wet-furred cat rained on by death;
its grey rubber mouth showing one sharp tooth;
paws rigid; it seemed to be snarling or laughing
at the great waste of deposited love.)

I knew a bank, also, where an ice plant once grew
where sleeps the memory of Rory Flett
whose life was found to be a useless growth
removable by gunshot. Death among the purple ice plant
with its magical juice running like blood through the narrow-
    hearted people-deep town
of wet clay and white stone, alkaline,
calcium carbonate,
in pharmacological form an aid to the digestion.

So all that murderous night the townspeople drank their stone
    Post Office, their Town Hall, their Opera House,
their small squat stone morgue by the green weed-waving
    river,
the white stone mill manufacturing flour.
The drank the walls, the towers, the prison, the stone doors
    and floors,
to neutralise the excess death,
the acid reality too corrosive for a town to swallow and live.

They survived. The ice plant made a purple blossoming
    camouflage of the dead.
The stone bees flew alive out of the carved walls of Bee
    Supplies Ltd the Best Honey.
The Mayor who had consumed the Town Hall
gazed with his mildly alkaline eyes,
his face statistically chalk-white
his stomach mayoral,
keeping his own council.

Rory Flett, Harry Sturm, Grandfather, Aunt Kate, my
    estranged mother,

my quiet father, when I undertake my daughter's death
    education
what will she make
of this curious history of my life?
Of Selwyn who also died though his death has not settled.
Of Talbot Edelman, the lonely nude I.
Of the dead novels and poems, the murdered words
for which I could never afford a decent burial;
the volcanoes whose lava buried another life in me, cities I
    never knew,
sparkling cities with towers and jewels; the earthquakes which
    divided me, my time, my life, my sex,
my breathing into and out of,
my take and give,
my loyalty and treason of lung;
live and die; the jewel; the dual; the duel
with witnesses and chosen weapons.

Heterodon Platyrhinos who plays dead.

The detachment sloughing off the skin of attachment,
the last adhesive, either love or death, that after a lifetime
    of taking,
learns to give.

23

Talbot Edelman and Daughter Buffalo—they and I—
have suddenly become We. How good it is to be not-I.
The spring of a clock has made a final whirring sound in my
   head.
Sawdust runs through my glass body. I catch at the sleeve
of something, someone hurrying by with their polished springs
   tightly coiled in their head,
their heart on the beat, knock-knock the full-memoried there
who have kept fast hold of the concentration of their lives
while I
gave everything away
to a passing importunate year.

Dear shoulder at the stopped wheel,
dear nose at the worn grindstone,
dear best foot going at last backward,
dear hand's incorrect confused turn,
dear hand faltering on the short road to mouth,
dear foot put down, still on earth,
dear moistened eyes,

I, Turnlung, go down and back with heart and hand and
    mouth and foot
and I turn with lung as Janus turns at the New year.

Are your parents living?
Are your parents living?
Haven't we met before?
Haven't we met before?
I know you,
dog, man, woman, buffalo,
I know you from somewhere,
your faces are familiar.
We have met before.
Are your parents living?
What are your names?

I had a friend called Selwyn. We were young and old
    together, and he died.
His heart was arrested.
He was arrested once in a men's lavatory
and he came to me and he cried,
and he said, All those men with ammonia in their eyes
and rusted tapwater dripping from their tools
and salt-corroded soles of their feet; and there was this cop in
    disguise.
O Selwyn had been around. He knew heartbreak.
He will go down in history, as far as the basement
where murders are committed in the weekend and the care-
    taker cleans up the vomit;
and he will go up in the world beyond the sweet executive
    sky to heaven.

He and I learned American from the picture shows in our
    town.
I was a chartered accountant.
He worked in the Grain Merchant's, telling wheat
everything it wanted to know. Together he and I travelled to
    that magnificent city, Hollywood,
a place full of bloodberries, presaging a bitter winter,
valleys full dimpled shirleys,
blond skies curled with cloudy ringlets,
bearded baddie hills violent with gun-thunder;
an oasis of dream of the edge of a yellow desert nightmare
until the rattlesnakes came to town;
Tongues grew thirsty, sharp as cactus,
phalluses hot, thicker than lit king cigars—
oh what a life we had—adultery for breakfast, divorce for
    dinner,
a lodging at Forest Lawn, the best motel.

We spent our days being mixed with the families of others,
    being, as the years passed,
the sweet hired help, the uncles who weren't uncles, the
    goodnatured
gentlemen who babysat and washed the nappies and had
long confidential talks with the wife, woman to woman;
and it was all comradeship after the manner of Walt
    Whitman.

Sometimes foundering women were caught in our innocently
    baited hook,
and went away with their lives bleeding, saying No, no, it
    doesn't hurt,

though I've seen them later with an ugly scar across their
    mouth
and some words, beyond repair, that cannot get out.

Our life was full of joy.
Once I began to put words in their place and perspective I
    was free.
I bundled in jewel, dual, duel, death, all the rest,
and they lived happily together in their comradely way.

Later in life, I thought, It is good to die. Who will teach me
    to die?

I knew that families, mothers and fathers and children and
    their pets all died.
I knew there was no special sexual or religious or racial
    qualification for death.
I said to die is to be complete,
and once I caught sight of God with his head in a cloud of
    thought
and his feet on the wet concrete floor of a men's toilet,
and I knew that differences fall away like used cells, taken by
    passing years,
the world finds good fertile soil in our lives;
beasts, men, insects, buildings, trees and terraces grow out of
    our skin,
firmly rooted, blossoming, fruiting,
and we are one and the same,
unique yet redundant,
we at last have ourselves to spare after all that use and growth,
and beware those who imagine it is the time they have to
    spare—called Leisure.
(Their delusion encourages them to build Leisure Villages!)

Time has no time to spare.
The true Leisure Village has a roof of flesh, body vents,
eye-windows,
while all those carefully paved paths have their directions
    affirmed
by the flesh hands that point the way to the hot salt pool,
the milk baths, the bearded forest
where a company of angels, unnoticed before, suddenly
  clarified like the sight of morning
emerging whole from light-birth
in a sparkle of dew and blood
will be on hand on mouth on lips in the forefront of the mind
    and deep in the heart
and in the bones, nesting in the golden marrow on a chalk-
    satin bed of strontium ninety.

How much the aged are to spare!
Death, rummaging,
gets the spare people for a song or less than a song,
a silence
or as Talbot Edelman would say, a Sanctuary.
Talbot Edelman has talked to me of the foetus brains,
of the wildernesses where the marshbirds go
to tangle with the wild rushes and the generous air and sky
in a web of sanctuary.

Are your parents living?
Are your parents living?
Mine are dead.
My father kept a grocery store in the country town of stone
    quarries.
We were poor because money ran like rice through his fingers.
He sold three kinds of oatmeal:

fine, medium and coarse.
The middle-aged people bought the coarse oatmeal for their
    constipation,
also, 'a little of the fig syrup, please.'
  Our clothes were always drenched in the dry snows of white
    and brown flour,
we lived through a storm of foodstuffs that escaped and settled
    anywhere but in the mouth, we lived in a whirlwind of
cereals before they were caught and cardboarded by commerce.
My father could go out in the street and shovel a townful of
    wheat for the fowls of the town.
The eggs we sold were always warm with fowl-droppings and
    one or two matted feathers on the shell.
My mother baked cakes and gingerbread dolls in the coal oven.
The bees buzzed by the windowpanes and the purple flowers
and we thought, with amazement, of their honey.

Are your parents still living?

And there was the cat.
Grandfather.
Rory Flett.
La cimetière triste de La Semillante.

Grandfather's rimless glasses,
the trimly made beds of the dead in the cemetery,
the crowns of jewels, the duels with witnesses, the dual lives,
the sooty geraniums,
and then, gradually, a way of life
a house of words by the sea
and my friends the dead writers and their words, witnesses,
    companions,
nurses who removed some of the arrows from my flesh.

And there was Selwyn who stayed.
Make no mistake, the majority
of beams of light and shy creatures and love-offerings
does not stay.

Man, dog, buffalo, do I know your name?
Laboratory dogs and tiny multiplying white mice with pink
skin,
please retain your differences until you are dead,
Be what you are. Let man and woman alone as man and
woman.
Be the distinguisher
not the extinguisher by the revelations of your nature;
for you do not know who your parents are or if they are living;
some of us, also, may not know
but we know that we do not know
and I would never presume, like the poet, to call the
hare at morning 'happy'.

Nor the mad, nor the dead.
Happiness is taken secretly, like love,
and almost never known for what it is,
though heard of, rumoured, sought at the end of the maze,
bound invisibly to the drowning stone
to the frozen honey of the stone bees.

A word for my daughter, flesh of my flesh,
my mind on Reptile Hall and Central Park Zoo.
Remember, daughter, I at last have custody of you.
You and Talbot Edelman are my family.
You will be brought up like a hoofed lady
to dance attendance on all the sky you can bear witness to,
and none will approach you with weapons,

my Daughter Buffalo

Tonight I sleep long, learning to play dead,
here among the funeral hearths and homes
where the bright welcoming fire burns
where the showman prepares his finishing touch
with a flame-burst of discreet artistry; too late.

The chromosomal message reached me
long ago, in the sanctuary, the place of stone bees and men
who place reliance on the noon sun,
where beasts lie warm but have no shadow
and ice is at last unknown.

Soon I shall sleep long. My inheritance shall be
to the family who surprised me on the border of Senility
who completed my death education by loving me
in the manner suited to the time and place of their lives,
a time unrepeatable as the genetic message
which Talbot Edelman spoke of:
                                    For him and Daughter
                                    Buffalo, I leave
what I have not, what I have not had, and what I have.

24

I took a cab to Thirty-fourth Street. Turnlung's landlady whose hair, I noticed, was sandy-coloured like the sand in the painting which now occupied my 'gap', opened the door almost at once in answer to the bell although she did not unfasten the chain lock.

'What is it?' she asked in the kind of Scottish accent which I am told is not heard in Scotland but which grows like an offshoot into the voices of the Scottish immigrants, killing year after year the otherwise hardy American sprouts.

'I've come to see Turnlung,' I said.

'Who are you?'

'A doctor.'

I said the word 'doctor' because I had learned to use the prestige of my profession for my own ends, reasoning that it was there free so why should I not use it. I was worried about Turnlung. I had dreamed about him almost every night since our last meeting, dreams peopled also by my parents, Lenore, Sally, reptiles, wild creatures caged in zoos, and cats and horses as jungle predators; in bizarre settings and situations, the more so because I had not known myself to be a prolific dreamer.

'A doctor?'

I was not prepared for the effect my announcement of myself would have on Turnlung's landlady. She gave a small cry. 'I've been waiting for you.'

As she still made no attempt to unfasten the chain lock I showed her the equivalent of an ID card. She looked shrewdly at me and at the card, then she unlooped the chain, sabotaging all her experience and caution as she said, 'You look like a doctor.'

'I phoned you,' she said.

'Me?'

'Well, you're the doctor. His room is on the fourth floor facing the garden.'

'I know,' I said, impressed with my knowledge and savouring the memory of it. All would be well now, I thought. I would help Turnlung, I would take care of him in his final erosion.

I was already hurrying up the stairs and to my surprise the landlady followed me, talking. 'Yes, it's a Mr Turnlung, doctor. A visitor to this country. I think he's a writer. Taps with his typewriter all day. This is the day I change his linen, doctor. I always change both sheets, never top to bottom as some do; even if you're not actually lying on it you can't have your body next to a sheet all week and not soil it. They say that every twenty-four hours the body gives off...' She stopped abruptly as she said 'body' and put her hand over her heart.

'So you see I knocked to change his sheets and there was no answer and at first I thought he was having a wee nap and hadn't heard me and I knocked louder, and then I opened the door and there he was, on the bed. I phoned the authorities. And here you are, the doctor.'

With the last sentence she caught up with me and together

we stood on the small landing outside Turnlung's room.

The front doorbell rang.

'That could be the ambulance,' she said, seeming not to know whether to doubt or to accept my evident efficiency in getting aid. She hurried downstairs, still without having told me about Turnlung, and a few minutes later I heard heavy footsteps and two ambulance men appeared, carrying a stretcher, while the landlady, breathless, hurried after them. As they pushed past me the landlady pointed to me as if to a significant monument. 'He's the doctor.'

All looked respectful and stood aside then, to let me go into the room before them. I had not yet become blase about the way in which my profession was acknowledged and respected everywhere—in shops, in planes, at parties, in the street by the children who called, 'Hey, Doc, Hey, Doc,' with affection in their voices. (I had yet to meet the rage of the large number of people whom the medical profession had failed.)

I went over to Turnlung's bed. We stood in a group around it, like extras hastily summoned to appear in the last scene of a film, an improvised family come to mourn the dead Turnlung, and to speculate in stage conversation about his last words, for Turnlung was dead. The landlady had thought he was unconscious; she had been afraid to investigate. I knew that he was dead; he had apparently died in his sleep.

The ambulance men waited for me to make some examin-ation, some statement. They watched as, using their equipment, I made the usual examination. Inwardly I was amazed at the way I so readily became an impersonal minister to the dead, the fact that the dead was Turnlung—Turnlung!—not seeming to affect my calm. I covered his face, and mysteriously urged to follow the conventions of a scene from a film, I turned slightly towards the group and slowly shook my head. My lips moved, also within a convention, 'soundlessly'. Then suddenly I uncovered his face. I had a wild hope that he would recognise me and speak to me. He was Turnlung.

A flutter of an eyelid, a movement of the lips, of the hand, seem such inadequate signs of life beside the abundance of life—the singing, shouting, running, leaping, flying, thinking, wanting, loving—that we demand from ourselves and others; we forget that the eyelid has only to be blinked, the hand to be lifted, for there to be proof. Again I covered Turnlung's dead face.

'Take him to the city mortuary,' I said, 'as an indigent.'

Not questioning my authority they proceeded to obey me. The city mortuary had been their destination in any case.

'He has no relatives in this country,' I said, disowning him. When the ambulance men had gone the landlady looked greedily around the room.

'His things,' she said, trying to suppress her excitement.

'They'll go to his Embassy or whatever representative he has in this country,' I said.

'The rent, then,' the landlady said, on her determined voyage of getting.

I gave her ninety dollars for the month.

'A death is more,' she said, rather unwillingly. 'Because the room's harder to let when they know. To be fair, it's not as hard as with a murder, especially a battering.'

I gave her fifty dollars for the death.

'Are you sure he has no relatives?' she asked. 'He spoke of a daughter living near Central Park. He has custody of her.'

'I'll see she gets his manuscripts,' I said, picking up a folder of papers. 'And I'll be in touch with his Embassy or Consulate. They will give the news to any friends he may have in his own

187

country. He was a well-known old man.'

'But not rich.'

'Not rich.'

'There's no money in it, then,' the landlady said. 'The police will be back. They'll want to *seal the room*.'

She spoke with emphasis looking at me as if to say, If you don't leave now you too will be *sealed*. I noticed she wore an unusual number of tassels on her clothing. Tassels drooped from her sleeves, bordered the ornamental V shape across her bosom, and encircled her throat in a terraced necklace, glass-tasselled like a chandelier. I felt there to be some impropriety in her wearing a necklace before noon.

'I'll see you out,' she said, closing and locking Turnlung's door.

I suspected that the shock of the death had prompted her to put herself in the stereotyped role of landlady, as I knew from Turnlung that she was not a typical landlady, that she had other interests besides cleaning, complaining, getting and gossip. She would be accustomed to death among her tenants, I thought, and the hint of briskness and festivity that she now showed could be an expression of her relief that this time she'd had an apparently 'natural causes' death, and not beating, rape or decapitation.

'He was a quiet man and he paid his rent,' she said as she opened the front door and I went out into the street. Her words were an epitaph of praise from one whose first two commandments were: Pay thy rent, and Keep thyself to thyself.

The shock of Turnlung's death was inducing me to behave like an automaton. Where only a few days before I had been thinking of the way in which the senile retain a supply of tourist phrases for use when everything about and within them is

suddenly foreign, I now found myself drawing my thoughts
from conversational phrases in a foreign land.

'You appear sad.'

'I am sad. My friend has died.'

'Was he a member of your family?'

'Yes, he was a member of my family.'

'Is your grandfather dead?'

'My grandfather has died.'

'Did your friend die suddenly or was it a prolonged illness,
with fever?'

'His temperature was normal.'

'Did you fetch the doctor?'

'I am the doctor.'

'Good morning, doctor. I hope it is not serious. Will the
patient live?'

'I am grieving over the death of my friend.'

'Where is the body?'

'The body is in the city mortuary.'

'Are there not private funeral establishments?'

'My friend was poor.'

'What was his income?'

'He had very little income.'

'Some men have great wealth. Was he not a banker? Do you
know where I may find a banker to cash in his traveller's
cheque?'

'The body will be moved to the hospital for dissection.'

'Do you know where I may find a lawyer to settle the will?'

'Five blocks to the north, by the railway station, next to the
phone booth.'

'Are there any rest rooms nearby?'

'There are rest rooms, a department store which sells
stationery, a drugstore, a restaurant, many other varieties of

stores where you may purchase gifts, clothes, leather handbags, postcards, and tickets for the opera.'

'I will go to the opera this evening. When is the funeral?'

'The body will be disposed of at the hospital.'

'Was it an infectious disease? I have been vaccinated against cholera and smallpox. I have a sore throat and earache and I would like to visit the doctor to get a prescription.'

'I am the doctor.'

'Good morning, doctor. I would like a prescription to take to the pharmacy. Where is the pharmacy?'

'The pharmacy is next to the bank where you may cash a traveller's cheque and near the department store where you may buy a leather handbag, a watch, a radio, and postcards.'

'I am deeply grieved that your friend has died in a foreign land.'

From the time I left Thirty-fourth Street to my arrival at my apartment my mind was occupied with bizarre thoughts and phrases and when I recovered a little and the phrases vanished, the resulting emptiness in my mind was quickly filled with shame for having rejected Turnlung and disposed of him as an indigent. I found the number of his Consulate, and phoned, and the secretary who answered said I could not speak to the Consul as he was on duty only at certain hours because the Consulate was shared with other nations who divided the rent among them. Or how, she asked, did I think they could afford to keep offices in central Manhattan?

I mentioned Turnlung, and when she said the name was unfamiliar, I asked her to find it in a reference book of his country. I mentioned his writings, *First Death* and so on. It just happened, she said, there was a literary expert, a professor, in the office at that moment, and she would consult both

the reference book and the professor. And would I wait?
I waited.

Five minutes later when she returned to the phone she told
me that the name *Turnlung* was completely unknown, and the
books I mentioned were unheard of and had never been
published.

'He's dead. But he's dead,' I told her, and tears came to my
eyes. 'Perhaps you know about making arrangements for
having a body shipped to your country?'

'*Shipped?*' She sounded horrified. 'Shipped? Just a moment.
Do you have his passport number?' I gave her the passport
number which I had. After a few moments she returned again
to the phone. 'Our government has no such passport, no such
number, and no such person.'

Her denial was defensive and full of fear. 'If you wish to
discuss the matter further you must come to the Consulate
in person,' she said abruptly, putting down the phone.

It seemed then that if there was a question of Turnlung's
reality, of his belonging anywhere, then he must belong only
to the bewildered buffalo and myself. I phoned the city morgue
which houses a crematorium where the indigents are disposed
of. I identified myself as a doctor. I inquired after Turnlung.

'There are so many,' the attendant said. 'This is only the
day before the weekend and we're already overstocked.' His
voice had the correct supermarket tone.

I gave him particulars of Turnlung's death and removal to
the mortuary, and I told him I had the papers necessary (which
I had) to transfer him to the research department of the
hospital.

The tone of a salesman came again into his voice; an awareness of the strength of the seller's market. 'He may have been
taken,' he said. He might almost have said in the next sentence,

'Apartments in that district are scarce, no sooner advertised than rented.'

I knew from experience that dead indigents were a physiological fortune with their death bequeathing to their body a rich adventurous future. How often in my last years as a medical student, I had waited at the mortuary for news of the latest accident and condition of the vital organs of the victim! I waited while the attendant found Turnlung's body.

'You're in luck,' he said. 'Old. Natural causes. Nobody's inquired. Most of the hospitals are busy with the two-car crash we had last night, seven killed, all under twenty, all with perfect hearts, eyes, kidneys, brains. And all'—his voice changed to a whisper over the phone—'all orphans!'

His voice became formal again. 'I'll see that Mr Turnlung is kept until you make arrangements for him. You'll bring your papers with you of course.'

I arrived at the mortuary and was immediately bathed in the Lysol-layered smell of death, and my breath escaped in a cloud of icy vapour when the attendant slid open the refrigerated drawer and drew aside the shroud to let me see Turnlung's face. I gazed at him. I could not find the Turnlung I knew, though no one had 'touched him up' to try to preserve him for relatives, arriving from a distance, who might not be able to persuade their memories to conjure an acceptable image of the vanished life; no one had rejuvenated him with mortuary cosmetics to make him appear to be on the verge of sitting up and demanding an explanation. I could feel only the dead weight of his death and the sense that it was dragging to itself, away from me, my memories of Turnlung. When I had last seen him alive he, with his symptoms of approaching senility, had claimed from me a concern to which, I was ashamed to own, I had been reluctant to give a practical form.

Now, in his new state, he was demanding from me all my knowledge of him, my memories, my dreams, with a successful trick of haulage that I tried to resist. Where were the thoughts about death which I had hoped to prize from *him*? His face gave me no message.

I felt cold anger. 'It's the one,' I said, in a manner of a victim identifying the criminal.

The attendant slid the drawer into the refrigerator; there was a purring sound as the motor adjusted to the change in temperature, I could see the rows of corpses, like produce not yet sold and I could not help feeling a kind of reflected prestige from Turnlung who, lying among the indigents, the 'unsold', had at last been 'taken'.

The attendant led me to the office where I showed my papers and signed the necessary forms.

'There's a high expectancy rate this weekend,' he said. 'After the formalities, police and so on, we might have just managed yours by noon tomorrow.'

By 'managed' he meant disposed of in the crematorium. The way he said 'yours' implied that he had discharged all responsibility toward Turnlung and was being relieved of a burden.

'We'll deliver him by the shuttle service,' he said, and there was a note of excitement in his voice as he added, 'Is it heart, lung, kidney? Eyes? Brains are in great demand lately. By the way, he wasn't anyone I'd be likely to know, was he? Did you know him? Didn't you say something about a *friend*?'

'No, no. I've never seen him before in my life,' I said.

As I was leaving he said in an undertone, talking out of the corner of his mouth and looking absurdly like the gangsters in the old movies then in fashion, who say, 'Don't move, I've

got you covered,' or 'One false move and you're dead.'
'We feel these things you know, deep down.'

25

I walked home to my apartment. It was hot in the street. Stagnant summer had arrived and the smell was of gasoline and gas leaks, rubber, tar, indefinable chemicals, with currents of the smell of brake fluid swirling around the street corners. There was no sky. The eastern cloud-lid fitted exactly around the rim of the city's horizon, with the pressure rising within, and the bursting point close. When I walked into the hallway of my apartment building, out of the bath of tar and cooking gas, I entered the luxuriously icy atmosphere reserved for the dead in the mortuary, and I was reminded of the fact of Turnlung's death. I don't think I had grasped the *fact* before then.

I could not mourn, I could not cry, I'd had so little education in death that I did not know how to deal with it. I found it hard to think of our love, even to remember it, yet I wanted to remember it, and the effort of searching for it in my mind was so great that I became exhausted. I lay down on the sofa and looked out at the pseudo-sky that was striped with yellow, with a fume-cloud like a poisonous puff ball swelling to the south. The leaves of the trees in the park were already being bled of their colour and were turning grey. In the distance I could see the wintry outline of the suffering elms, where their disease had burned and scarred them, and I thought of how in the towns where the elms had lined the streets, maples were now being planted in the shade of the elm-corpses or the corpses they would become when the disease had finally spread through their body, how the young maples in their first fall had made a firelight of leaves up and down the avenues beneath the doomed elms which were now little more than obstructions, protected in their last days only by some aboreal charity and pity in the hearts of a few councillors.

As I lay on the sofa my feeling grew that I was living in a foreign land, that the lives and death I was knowing were not mine. I felt as if I had given up my life, that it had been intimations only, addressed to me, which I had refused at last and distributed in the streets of the city. I looked along the avenues of the dead elms, at the maple leaf-light on my grandfather's face, and at the treasured view of the woods which he could not see as he watched the beaming of a nightmare programme from the sky.

I fell asleep. My mind was crowded with thoughts of people whom I suppose I would call my 'blood' people, and my *own* people who being accessible to me beyond the conforming structure of the genetic code thus gave me the illusion of having a 'will' of my own. It was a dream. The people were neither departing nor meeting a traveller yet they crowded into my dream as into a transport terminal, and I watched as they became an ordered assembly with my blood kin on one side and my life kin on the other, like families of the bride and the groom seated at a wedding ceremony, and, as at a wedding, I saw the critical glances that each side gave to the other. There was a murmuring, buzzing, such a sound of swarming that at first I imagined the assembly was of bees disguised as people. In my dream I put my hand to my face and I realised I was wearing a bee mask to protect myself while my hands were encased in heavy gloves such as apiarists wear during a swarm; and then I thought perhaps I was a baseball player preparing myself for my weekly game, yet that idea was confusing, for I had never been a baseball player, though my teachers and my parents had hoped that I would 'grow out of' whatever interested me then, and 'grow into' baseball. I suddenly felt the desolation of the place that is in childhood between 'growing out of' and 'growing into' and it seemed that all my childhood had been spent there, in a no-child's land of no departure and no arrival.

The assembly was diminishing. I stood before them. I could identify them as being a few people I knew, a few animals, and the others—the unknown and known dead, the unborn and born dead, the sick, the incomplete in mind and body with an incompleteness which like the deliberate errors made in some forms of Eastern art may signify perfection and humility. I could see my dog Sally looking very canine and matronly with her removed organs arranged, preserved, beside her, almost as some middle-aged women like to display their gallstones, and middle-aged men their kidney stones. Sally stared at me with her one eye, giving no sign that she recognised me. And there was Lenore, very tall with blond light in place of hair, like one of the bathers in the painting of *Noon*. She had two of her small patients, one on each side, holding fast to her hand and gazing trustfully at her, and now and again they too became mere stripes and blades of light as in the scene on the beach. Thinking that I may have been watching an enactment of the Noon scene I glanced again at Sally and I was relieved to see that the expression on her face was without that furious rage. I said to myself, in my dream, 'Rage is absent from her,' and hearing myself say it I felt it was a pronouncement, as after a surgical operation, that I had removed Sally's rage.

Lenore was looking at my mother who sat in the opposite group with my father, my brother, and, or so I surmised the treelike forms to be, my shadowy ancestors. Apart from my parents, on their side, my grandfather sat dressed in the clothes of another age. He had my build, my face, my eyes, my skin and as he and I stared at each other I felt him to be ransacking me of my physical and emotional characteristics and I decided, for I still thought of myself as an apiarist about to hive a swarm of bees, that I should capture my grandfather first.

I knew that we were all standing under the sky yet I had the impression of being confined within a space bounded by stone walls and a sky of stone. I looked down at my hand in its outsized red glove. I wanted to stretch it out to touch the sky and the apparent grey stone, and knowing I could not, and that I would never reach it, I was overcome by a feeling of sadness and regret that I would never know if the sky were air or stone. It was not the city sky nor was it the Siberian sky of my other dreams of my grandfather, not the pleasant summer sky of my father's paintings, nor the pale sick sky of the painting of Noon. I remember that I stood in front of the assembly, trying not to panic, desperately trying to 'place' the sky while the assembly waited for the event to begin. What was the event to be? I wondered. How I wished I could touch the sky! My hand in its glove could be versatile. As well as capturing bees surely it could touch skies? My heart beat faster with confusion and fear as I gazed again at the enormity of the marble canopy; here and there it was blue and grey with a pink flush like pink marble. I thought that it seemed to be curiously like a membrane seen from within; like the tissue, perhaps, of the placenta; then the pink flush would be blood. But why were my gloves red if I had not reached out and touched? Was I trapped within a stone membrane? Was I also of stone in the midst of a swarm of stone bees?

The heaviness, the anchoring factor of anxiety dreams as opposed to the orgasmic floating-flying of the release of tension, came upon me and I found I could not move. Just then my grandfather, the image of myself, stood up and announced in Russian which everyone, even I, understood, that the event was about to begin. I could see fear in the faces. Why were they afraid? My grandfather then asked all to prepare their bids, warning them not to move unless they were bidding. There was no catalogue, he said, apologising, but the auction was being held at short notice.

The humming and murmuring ceased. The critical glances of one side towards the other continued. I wondered why I persisted in the thought that the people were bees as they lacked wings and surcingles and I could neither see nor feel their stings, and there was no evidence of honeycomb or honey. In alarm I put my hand to my face to reassure myself it was there. I could feel nothing.

I heard one of the auction attendants say, as over someone who is dying, 'He can feel nothing, nothing at all.'

I cried out, 'Deep down, deep down.'

No one could hear me.

My grandfather, with my build, my voice, my skin, my eyes, began to speak. 'Much has changed hands privately.'

I glanced down at my gloved hands, suddenly doubtful if I possessed hands.

As I watched the bidding I began to realise that I could no longer hear. I could see the movements of the crowd—a lifted arm, a waved hand, which showed that bidding was brisk and all were bidding except Sally who slept with her head between her paws. Occasionally she wagged her tail, and I smiled to myself as I thought this might be mistaken for a bid, and then I realised it was a bid, and that whatever Sally had wanted she had succeeded in getting.

Suddenly I thought of Turnlung and his daughter buffalo. I searched for them in the crowd. If he were here, I thought, he would explain everything, he would give me safety, sanctuary, he would unmask and unglove me and remove me from this place of stone sky and stone bees, he would help me escape through these membranous walls. He and Daughter Buffalo and I would elope, like lovers, and though the rest of the world would pursue us with weapons and witnesses, nothing would be able to hurt us. But where would we go? And where was Turnlung? And what if Daughter Buffalo's prairie were being put up for auction?

The bidding continued. I could hear nothing now. I might have had ears of stone.

Turnlung does not care, I thought. He keeps his secret of death.

I saw him, in my dream, within my dream, lying in the top drawer of my mother's dressing table, a tiny Turnlung like a doll, and I'd been sneaking into my mother's room, had opened the drawer, and looked down on Turnlung with his blue painted open eyes, then shut the door quickly and tiptoed out, and I'd run into the woods near the lake and a red cardinal followed me, dropping blood as it flew, and the blood hung in shapes like clothing along the lower branches of the trees, and the crows flew wildly about, screeching, but one old crow sat coughing up his phlegm in the pine trees.

As the dream within the dream came to me I ralised that the clarity of the images had been enhanced by blindness. I knew that I was blind, and I could see only within myself. I could no longer see nor hear the auction, and sensing that however incomplete I might be now, it was I who was being auctioned, and I would never know who—man, beast, woman, God—had bid for me, I tried to retain one last image to keep within me and myself, for all that remained to me now were images and sensations of swirling darknesses, cold mists, cold stone and marble and solid skin surfaces with a rare fur touch like a bee on its way to a flower, and a movement of air after it had passed, and once I thought I felt the wing of a marsh bird against my face, and then I thought with anger at Turnlung, But I am not an acquaintance of marsh birds.

I wondered where it was flying. Perhaps there was nowhere left for it to fly to. I wanted to call after it, 'Beware the New Jersey Marshes and the Great Bear Swamp.'

Then I knew that my sense and memory of colour had gone, no doubt auctioned in a miscellaneous lot marked Memory. I tried to piece together an image, to make one decipherable mark upon the map of darkness which I no longer knew to be darkness. I knew of my family, of Sally, of Lenore, of the dead Turnlung, only as sensations, moving or still presences, like currents in dark seas, not as obstacles of mass and form but as movement or as an excision of the idea of movement or the *lining* of the idea of movement which, in touch with a final nerve, was able to register at first simple hot and cold, then cold only, the cold of stone made fluid, bleeding blood without colour. I felt all flowing away from me as in an act of love, but, unlike in love, I could not follow, having no self to follow the stream. I was nothing, with the last curse upon me, that of uselessness.

To this day I remember my dream. I was dissolved, dispossessed, and I could not understand why. It had not been an act of punishment. In the early stages of my dream when I still had my eyesight I knew that Grandfather's glances at me were those of sympathy and love. I felt no hostility from my family nor from Sally and Lenore. Was it, then, their love for me which enabled them to remove my life from me, leaving me without one lasting image of my own, while (in my dream this occurred to me) the absent Turnlung and Daughter Buffalo gallivanted through the world of the dead, in the protective custody of death?

There was a time, in the dream, after all had been taken from me, when I rose to the verge of waking and could see and feel and think once again, and recalling the incidents of the dream, the stone walls and sky, myself in a field of stone bees, the auctioning of myself, forgetting the panic and resistance I had felt, I remembered that I knew a deep feeling of peace, and I remembered Turnlung's story of the two dogs which could not be separated from their loving, of the linesman locked to the electric impulse of death, of the adhesive embrace of the world of life, and of the dead who touch their cheek upon the calm undemanding cheek of stone that offers no promise to seize, strangle or make warm.

I woke from my dream with the sound of the airconditioner murmuring and buzzing in my ears. I thought of Turnlung, and of the dead Sally. I worried that in their death they might have no moment of sanctuary, therefore I leased part of my life and memory to them, where they remain, and where Daughter Buffalo grazes as if she grazed upon miles of prairie.

26

Late that summer both my parents died in an automobile crash. My brother and I sold our parents' home. Disposing of them and their possessions I became aware that they who had lived refusing to acknowledge or to befriend death had lived very close to its border with their lives packed, so to speak, for their departure immediately on summons. I felt it might have been accurate to say that their lives belonged strictly to death since their refusal to unpack into the world could have been evidence of their unwillingness to stay; and I was reminded of a maid we once had who had been afraid to unpack for fear she would be molested. My parents, fearing to be molested both by death and by life had lived with death in their hearts.

We auctioned the paintings my father had bought over the years, and when I attended the auction at a downtown gallery I wondered if my dream would have relevance. The gallery was soundproofed, the walls and ceilings lined with insulating material, the floors carpeted with deep-pile carpet, and when the auction began I half-expected, as in the dream, to be unable to hear the voice of the auctioneer, to see only as the bidders raised or moved an arm, nodded, beckoned, almost as if they were exchanging limbs and glances for paintings.

I need not have feared, however. I could both hear and see. The paintings, carefully catalogued, photographed and numbered, were sold one by one, and although the proceeds were to be divided between Benjamin and me I felt little interest in the price, only a sense of loss as I watched the attendant raise high an armless, legless painting, like a hoisted child, to give the clients a clearer view, and afterwards when the buyers claimed their paintings I had the same impression of the infantile helplessness within the paintings that I used to have when my father brought the paintings home, holding them as if they were being carried against their will, like infants upon whom he had forced parentage in an afternoon's shopping.

I was glad, at the last moment, to be able to retrieve the painting *Noon*, which had mistakenly been listed in the catalogue and for which a private buyer had already promised to pay well above the reserve price. Only two days after my parents' death an agent for the buyer had written describing the painting in intimate detail and expressing a wish, a 'desperate wish' to own it. His description of the painting had made me uneasy as it was very close to my assessment of it and the impact of it on me, which I had discussed with no one. When I asked the gallery director to name the buyer he could give no details, only that he was from abroad and wished to remain anonymous.

My parents died and were disposed of in no time, although they clung, as the dead do, to living memory, slowly relinquishing their hold as each day passed, at night returning to inhabit the borders of dreaming until these, too, were closed against them, and they grew accustomed to their permanently exiled state. As material bodies my parents had willed themselves for medical research, and thus were swiftly dispatched to the Laboratory of the Geriatric Department where my Death Department was housed, and, without knowing it, I may have lectured upon the ageing tissues in my mother's and father's bodies. Their brains were removed to our Brain Museum where they stood in labelled jars (Edelman Brain) upon the shelves near such relics as the Croxby Tumour (quite famous in its day), the Butor Brain (also a medical curiosity) and the routine Fleishmann's Tumour. In spite of my dream of wholesale disposal of myself I had actually collected some handsome trophies of people and animals I had known, with the exception of the one which I longed most to possess—Turnlung. When I inquired at the laboratory, even though I had supervised delivery of him personally, I was told he had never been heard of and could not be traced, that no such body or person had been received, which angered me for I have always been in full possession of my faculties, a reasoning man not given to fantasy. When I phoned the city mortuary they too denied knowledge of Turnlung. I asked to speak to the attendant who had interviewed me and who had whispered, as I left, 'We feel these things deep down,' and he too denied all knowledge both of Turnlung and of having spoken to me or shown me a body.

That time of my life was suddenly full of sadness: my parents dead, the home sold, the paintings auctioned; Sally gone, Lenore gone, Turnlung gone; all that remained was my apartment and my death studies. After the shock of my visit one day to Thirty-fourth Street in search of Turnlung's room and my inability to find or recognise the house, it became my habit to walk there in the weekends in the hope that I might discover someone who knew Turnlung or his landlady. Many of the houses in the street had been condemned and were being demolished and the air was so full of stone-dust that each time I walked the length of the street I emerged as from a stone-storm, with grey deposits in my hair, my clothes, and on my skin. No one remembered or had known Turnlung. Soon, when I asked, they began to look at me with suspicion and disbelief. Nothing remained of him. My only triumph was in recognising the Funeral Homes which still stood in the district and were, to me, evidence of the veracity of my memory.

I walked also in Central Park Zoo, enquiring about the buffalo, the young female who had been six months old that summer. The attendant, newly employed, said he believed there had been a female buffalo but it had been removed from the zoo that summer, transferred somewhere, maybe stolen, he added facetiously.

'She could be frolicking on the prairie,' he said.

Old Mother Buffalo still gazed out with bewildered gloom from her enclosure. She had aged many years in a few weeks of summer. I asked the attendant why they didn't shoot her, she appeared to be so unhappy.

'She's a valuable representative of the species,' he said importantly, with a facile pride that might have included in the same statement, 'She's a member of Congress, a friend of the first astronaut to walk on the moon.'

I stared at Mother Buffalo, trying to force her in some way to recognise me, to admit that Turnlung and I had visited her and her daughter, that Turnlung had been given custody of her daughter, with rights, privileges and responsibilities. Mother Buffalo obstinately gave no sign. She, as the others had done, dispossessed me of the memory of Turnlung.

The incidents I have written of took place ten years ago. I am still a young man. I am now Head of the Department of Death Education. My life since that summer has been ascetic and solitary and the closest I have been to love has been my involvement with death which, being a national involvement, should not therefore touch me more acutely, except that I, like the young mariner, have control of the crossbow or its equivalent, for use in my work.

I can no longer focus directly on loving. Women recognise me and avoid me, avoiding destruction. With my parents dead, I have as my only mother, the American Flag, and as my father, a fur-collared bathroom. My adopted Daughter Buffalo has gone or was only a dream. At times I do not know whether I am robbing or being robbed, loving or killing or bringing to birth, but I know peace, an escape from restlessness, from home, income, marketable lives, disposable deaths, when I walk through the wards where the old men lie contemplating death, and I remember Turnlung.

EPILOGUE

Yes, I am an old man, a traveller down Instant Street, with water in the corner of my eye and milkwhite seeing.

Yes, I move my arm like a rusted reap hook to clear away the undergrowth growing me under.

No, I have not tried to explain to anyone about my brief summer in a foreign land ten years ago, though I have talked of it often. There is time to talk here, in the nursing home where I have just celebrated my eighty-fifth birthday and there are listeners, not always attentive or credulous. One of my old friends, a writer five years younger than I, is always pleased to remind me, slyly, that as far as he knows I have never left my native land, 'except in imagination'. I have shown him the manuscript which I wrote, recording my impressions and memories, with Edelman's version of the time, the events, the dreams he dreamed, but he still remains sceptical of the reality, although, wisely, he has not tried to define 'reality'. In my long life I have grown used to the tendency of human beings to ransack one another's reality, and to the way they go about it, with all the cunning of jewel thieves. I hold fast to my reality.

It has not been easy. When, after returning here, I wrote to the Death Institute at Talbot Edelman's hospital in New York City, the letter was returned to me: Neither the Death Institute nor Talbot Edelman were known, according to the message written across the envelope. When each month I spend part of my meagre pension on a journal of medical studies in the hope of finding some reference to Talbot Edelman, or perhaps an article written by him, I do not lose hope when, again and again, I find no trace of him or of a reference to death studies. I have a clear memory and unclouded brain. I cling—you might say that I am *attached*—to the vivid memory of my time in New York and of my love for Edelman who, for me, though others may question this, was the 'typical American'.

My health is good. Most of the patients here are not patients as such, though all are aged and most are referred to as being 'ambulant', and one, I notice, in support or advertisement of this fact, carries a fine book of poems by one of our poets, entitled *Ambulando*. I have a private room and, according to the brochure which I studied before I came to live here, 'everything I wish'—that is, a locker, a television set, a wardrobe, my own bathroom. Future necessities, not openly discussed, are catered for: in the storeroom next to my wardrobe there are a brand-new wheel chair with brakes and steering device, a commode handsomely antique like a throne, and a sparkling bedpan that I swear you could mistake for sterling silver.

I do not write as often as I used to. On some days I write letters to Talbot Edelman in New York but I have given up posting them since my early ones were returned to the Dead Letter Office. I write verses also, about Reptile Hall, and Daughter Buffalo and Edelman and New York, and my room in Thirty-fourth Street among the Funeral Homes. And I think of my death education and my death diploma. And of words.

And of the word God. And as I grow older and more dependent on others I must spend my time protecting myself against the pilferers of my reality, and where once it was easy, my weapons were many, and my devices, now each day and night bring exhaustion for it is impossible to relax, even in dreams, for the dead lurk there, who would not have my memory as it is, who would enter it to make their own preferred deposits.

This home overlooks the sea, and, again according to the brochure, has 'a magnificent view'. The beach is near, a lovely beach in this land of lovely beaches, and as this is the subtropical north, the sun appears punctually, stays all day, and sets in splendour. As I write this I am sitting on a seat quite close to the beach. I wait for the nurse to fetch me out of this terrible noon sun. She has been delayed and though I am ambulant I can't walk on the uneven ground across to the buildings as I was once able to. Down on the beach there are a few figures like streaks of light in the water. The sky is pale, as if unwell. Looking down I see that I have no shadow. Nothing has shadows in this noon sun.

The waves are still, a vast tract as of a prairie or plain, or a savannah under Siberian skies. The streaks of light play upon the waves. It's hard to know if they are people or animals. In the foreground there's a small white dog like a flare of anger. I can feel the concentration of his rage as he stands with his back to the ocean, still as stone, furiously staring.

How still everything is! A murmuring. Is it my blood? Bees in a hive of honey? Animals? People? Small waves or grass?

I say to myself, 'Now. Now this is what I have.'

Whether I dreamed Talbot Edelman, the lonely nude I, Daughter Buffalo, the summer in New York, whether Talbot Edelman's story and mine, as set down, are of my own making, it does not matter. What matters is that I have what I gave; nothing is completely taken; we meet in the common meeting place in the calm of stone, the frozen murmurs of life, *squamata*, *sauria*, *serpentes*; in the sanctuary.